EXCHANGING A LEOPARD CAT FOR A PRINCE
—Famous Trials Conducted by Lord Bao

Translated by Sun Haichen

Foreign Languages Press   Beijing

First Edition 1997

ISBN 7-119-01896-5

© Foreign Languages Press, Beijing, China, 1997

Published by Foreign Languages Press
24 Baiwanzhuang Road, Beijing, 100037, China

Distributed by China International Book Trading Corporation
35 Chegongzhuang Xilu, Beijing, 100044, China
P.O. Box 399, Beijing, China

Printed in the People's Republic of China

Contents

Prologue   1

Interrogating a Buddhist Statue   3

Misadventures of a Fan Pendant   14

The Ghost in the Crock   22

The Case of the Woundless Corpse   36

Execution of the Marquis of Anle   52

An Interlocking Murder Case Uncovered by a Pig
Head   75

Exchanging a Leopard Cat for a Prince   98

Obtaining the Contract by a Hoax   154

Prologue

In China "Lord Bao" has been a household name for over 900 years, famous for his ingenuity in cracking difficult cases and his equity in enforcing the law. He has become the symbol of law and justice, and many of the trials he conducted have become part of Chinese folklore. Though all these stories are based on actual cases, supernatural elements have been added to account for Lord Bao's incredible ability to solve the most complicated cases.

We hope you will find each of the following stories gripping in plot and exhilarating in outcome.

Lord Bao, whose given name was Zheng, was born in 999 in the Northern Song Dynasty (960-1127). His face was so dark that he became known by the nickname "Blackface" and later, "Black-Faced Lord Bao." His family lived in Hefei, Anhui Province and was well-to-do and able to hire a private tutor for him. In his twenties, he bade his parents farewell and went off to the imperial capital, Kaifeng, where he passed the national civil service examination and became a "metropolitan graduate." He was now ready to embark on his career as a government official.

Interrogating
a Buddhist Statue

After obtaining the title "metropolitan graduate," Lord Bao stayed in the imperial capital, Kaifeng, waiting for an appointment. Soon he received papers from the court making him magistrate of Dingyuan County in Fengyang Prefecture, Anhui Province. He packed his luggage, tucked away his official papers, and set out with his servant, Bao Xing.

On entering the district of Dingyuan County, Lord Bao changed out of his official robe so he could obtain some information firsthand dressed as an ordinary traveler. They stopped to eat at an inn. Just then a man walked in and was warmly greeted by the waiter. "Haven't seen you for a long time, Mr. Pi!" The man sat down at the table next to theirs. The waiter went inside and soon returned with two pots of wine and two cups. The man looked up in surprise, "Hey! I am alone. Why do you bring two pots and two cups?" The waiter was staggered. "I saw someone behind you when you came in," he said. "His hair was all tangled and his face smeared with blood. So I thought you had just dragged him out of a fight, and the two of you were going to have a few drinks together. But now he's gone! Or maybe I just got dizzy in the head and didn't really see anything."

At these words, the man's face changed color. Without saying anything, he got up, paid for the wine, and went away in a hurry.

Lord Bao, who had taken in everything, asked the

waiter to come over. "Who is that fellow?" he asked.

"That's Pi Xiong, the leader of the 24 local horse peddlers. I don't know what's wrong with him today."

Lord Bao finished his meal and told Bao Xing to go to the magistrate's office to announce his arrival. Then he left the inn and walked leisurely down the street. By the time he arrived at the *yamen* (the government office), the runners and clerks had already lined up in front of the gate. He entered the office, exchanged papers with his predecessor, and accepted the magistrate's seal as well as all the files and documents. He immediately sat down and began to leaf through the case records of criminals which had been executed in autumn. When he came across a recent murder case about a man named Shen Qing charged with killing a monk in the Buddhist temple, he found the judgment unconvincing and decided to try the case again.

The runners, informed by Bao Xing that the new magistrate had traveled incognito to the *yamen*, all realized that Lord Bao must be a very astute and stern person and that they could not afford to neglect their duties. As soon as Lord Bao issued his order, the runners walked into the principal hall of the *yamen* in an orderly file and announced the opening of the trial in resounding voices.

Lord Bao sat down at his table and ordered Shen Qing to be brought in.

A short while later Shen Qing was taken from prison, brought into the hall, and relieved of his shackles.

Lord Bao looked at him closely. Shen Qing appeared to be in his early thirties, weak in physique, timid in expression, and trembling with fear. He did not have the look of a murderer.

"Shen Qing," said Lord Bao, "I am the new magistrate of Dingyuan. Now you must confess to me how you killed the monk in the temple, and you must tell nothing but the truth!"

Shen Qing looked up to see a new magistrate with a dark face and piercing eyes. Lowering his head, he began to speak in a sobbing voice.

"To answer Your Excellency's question: Your humble subject is Shen Qing, 28 years old, and a native of this county. On that particular day I was on my way back from a relative's. It was getting late, and it would not stop raining, so the road became very muddy. I was never very brave and dared not travel at night. When I reached the old Buddhist temple about three *li* (one *li*=1/2 kilometer) south of the county, I went in and stayed the night there. Early the next morning the rain stopped, so I left the temple and went on my way. Then I was stopped by two runners who came after me, and I told them that I had spent the night at the temple and was going home. They said I could not go but had to return with them to the temple to have a look, as there was a large bloodstain on my back. We entered the temple. Oh, my goodness! What should we see but a monk lying dead by the Buddhist statue! I really had nothing to do with it! However, the two runners brought me to the *yamen* and charged me with killing that monk. I am wronged! Your Excellency! I am wronged!"

Lord Bao thought for a moment. "When did you leave the temple?"

"Before dawn."

"Where did you get the bloodstain on you clothes?"

"It was too dark to see anything when I entered the temple that evening, so I just lay down by the statue. I didn't know what had happened there before that. Maybe the blood from the dead body flowed on the ground and that was how my clothes got stained. I didn't notice anything the next morning because I was still half asleep when I started off. Your Excellency, I am innocent!"

Lord Bao gazed at Shen Qing for a while. "Take him away," he ordered. Then he turned to Bao Xing. "Get the sedan chair ready! I am going to the Buddhist temple."

Lord Bao set off in the sedan chair and Bao Xing accompanied him, riding a horse. Lord Bao thought to himself, "Why didn't Shen Qing throw away the blood-stained clothes if he had killed the monk? Moreover, if he had killed the monk, he would have had a bloodstain on the front of his garment, not on the back. Finally, the monk seemed to have been killed with an axe, but Shen Qing was not carrying the weapon when he was seized, nor was it found in the temple."

As Lord Bao was thinking in this way, the sedan chair arrived in front of the temple. Telling the runners to stay outside, Lord Bao entered the temple accompanied only by Bao Xing. The main Buddhist statue was in a state of disrepair, and the minor statues on both sides had all collapsed. It was obvious that the temple had been abandoned for quite some time.

Lord Bao walked around the temple and looked everywhere, not saying a word. He turned to the back of the main statue and stared at it for a long time. Finally he nodded his head, as if well satisfied with what he had found. Looking down on the ground, he saw a pool of blood and traced it to a corner of the temple, where he bent down and picked up something. He looked at it and tucked it away in his sleeve. "Let's go," he said to Bao Xing. "There's nothing else for us to see here. We'll return to the office."

Back in his office, Lord Bao went to his studio where he sat down and had a cup of tea, his eyes closed as if napping. After a while he opened his eyes and called out to Bao Xing, "Who is the head runner on duty today?"

"Hu Cheng."

"Tell him to come in."

Hu Cheng entered and knelt in salute. "Hu Cheng pays respects to Your Excellency!"

"You may get up," said Lord Bao. "I have a question for you. Do we have carpenters in our county?"

"Yes, quite a few."

"Very good. I need some woodwork done urgently. Go out and find some carpenters for me and bring them in early tomorrow morning."

Hu Cheng received the order and went away at once to carry it out. At this Bao Xing was puzzled. "What kind of woodwork were you talking about, my lord?"

"Get the meal ready!" Lord Bao gave Bao Xing a glance that stopped him from asking any more questions. Bao Xing walked away awkwardly.

Holding the teacup in his hand, Lord Bao gazed at the fine picture on it and murmured to himself, "Tomorrow I will have a coffin made for the murderer!"

The following morning, Hu Cheng arrived. "Your Excellency, I have brought the carpenters. They are all waiting outside."

"Good. Get a few low tables ready and also prepare some ink and writing brushes. Take the carpenters to wait outside the rear salon. I will come in a few minutes."

Lord Bao washed his face and went to the rear salon with Bao Xing. He ordered the carpenters to be brought in.

There were nine of them altogether. Coming into the salon, they knelt to salute Lord Bao. "Your Excellency, your humble subjects pay their respects to you!"

"You may get up, all of you. I have invited you here because I need some shelves made to support my flower pots, and I want them to be novel-looking. Each of you will draw a picture of your design. Whoever comes up with the best design will get a handsome reward." Then he had the low tables with ink and writing brushes brought in.

The nine carpenters sat down at the tables and began to rack their brains, eager to please the magistrate with the most novel design. Some were used to drawing with a bamboo pen and were rather clumsy with the writing brush; some became nervous in front of the magistrate, and their hands trembled so much that they could hardly draw; some looked well at ease and, after thinking carefully, drew their pictures without hesitation.

His hands clasped behind him, Lord Bao walked around the carpenters one by one and watched them drawing with interest.

After a while all the carpenters had finished drawing the sketch for the shelves and handed it in one after another. Lord Bao took the sketches and looked at them. He turned to ask one of the carpenters, "What's you name?"

"My name is Wu Liang."

Lord Bao took another look at his sketch and murmured, "Very good!" Then he turned to the other carpenters, "You may go now. Wu Liang alone will stay."

After the other carpenters had left, Lord Bao said to Bao Xing, "Beat the drum to announce the opening of trial! Take Wu Liang to the principal hall!"

Having changed into his official robe, Lord Bao took his seat at the principal hall of the *yamen*. Wu Liang was brought before him.

Lord Bao slammed his wooden block down on the table and demanded in a harsh voice, "Wu Liang, why did you kill the monk? Confess your crime to save yourself from the birch!"

9

Wu Liang was flabbergasted. "Your Excellency, what's all this about? Who killed what monk? I am a law-abiding carpenter and have never done anything wrong! Please find out the truth about this!"

Lord Bao smiled coldly. "A law-abiding carpenter indeed! I knew you would not confess easily. However, the Buddhist statue in that temple told me last night that it was you, Wu Liang, who killed the monk. Do you still deny it?"

"Your Excellency, I am wronged!" said Wu Liang. "If, as you said, the Buddhist statue has accused me of murdering the monk, please let it confront me here in court!" Wu Liang thought to himself that a Buddhist statue could never speak and could not provide evidence against him.

Lord Bao broke into a smile on hearing this. He turned to the runners and issued an order. "Go to the temple and carry the statue here!"

The runners looked at one another in disbelief. "Your Excellency, did you say we are to bring the statue here?"

"Yes! Bring the Buddhist statue into this hall! Do it without delay!"

Not daring to say another word, the runners left in a hurry.

Soon the Buddhist statue was carried into the hall. Intrigued by the sight, people in the street swarmed to the yamen and waited outside the gate, wanting to find out how the new magistrate was going to interrogate a statue.

Lord Bao left his seat and walked to the statue. He whispered a few words, then listened attentively and nodded his head, as if enjoying a conversation with the statue. Some of the runners standing along the hall nearly burst out laughing. Even Bao Xing, who had served in Lord Bao's family for many years, did not know what Lord Bao was doing. "What trick is my master playing?" he could not help asking himself.

Lord Bao finished talking with the statue and returned to his seat. "Wu Liang," he said, "the Buddha just told me that when you killed the monk, you left a mark on the back of the statue."

Wu Liang again cried that he was innocent. Lord Bao told the runners, "Take him to the statue and check it out."

Wu Liang was taken to the back of the statue. Just below the right shoulder of the statue there was a bloody handprint—it was a left hand with six fingers. Wu Liang also had a six-finger left hand, and when it was brought down on the statue it matched the handprint perfectly. Wu Liang was terribly frightened. "My goodness!" the runners all murmured in amazement. "The magistrate must be a deity himself!"

Lord Bao had a severe look in his dark face. He brought down the wooden block and demanded loudly, "Wu Liang, what do you have to say?"

The runners roared in unison, "Confess at once! Confess at once!"

His face turning white with terror, Wu Liang said, "Please quiet your anger, Your Excellency, I will confess! I was friendly with the monk of the temple. He was fond of drinking, and I am also a drunkard. That day he invited me for a drink, but he got drunk first. I told him he'd better take on an apprentice to help him do some odd jobs; at his death he would also have someone to take care of his burial. The monk patted me on the shoulder and said, 'It is hard to find an apprentice these days. As for my burial, I don't need to worry about that. In the past few years I have saved over 20 taels of silver.' So I asked, 'Where do you keep the silver? If it should get lost, several years of effort will be wasted!' He said, 'No, it's quite safe! I've hid the silver where no one can find it.' 'Really?' I said.

'Is the place really that safe?' The monk placed both hands on my shoulders, and when he opened his mouth to speak, he smelled strongly of liquor. 'Brother, I will not keep it from you, but you must not tell this to anyone. I have put the silver in the head of the Buddha's statue.' Before that moment I had been talking with him without any ill intention. But when he mentioned the silver and revealed its hiding place, I became greedy and wanted to seize it."

Wu Liang paused to wipe the perspiration from his forehead.

"Go on!" ordered Lord Bao.

"Yes, Your Excellency! Afterwards, I said deliberately that it would be better to look into the head of the statue to see if the silver was still there. The monk staggered to his feet and leaned on my shoulder, saying he would take me there to have a look. By that time I could think of nothing but seizing the silver. As he was obviously very drunk, I decided to kill him with my axe. I was used to chopping wood with the axe, but when I raised it to strike the monk, my hands felt so weak that I missed him. When he saw the axe in my hands, the monk realized what was happening and tried to snatch it from me. I was then filled with panic, but I managed to throw him to the ground, and struck him repeatedly with the axe until he became totally motionless. I struggled to my feet, climbed up the statue and, holding the back of the statue with my left hand, I took out the silver from its head with my right hand. As it was already dark outside, I ran away from the temple without being seen. I didn't know that I had left my handprint on the back of the statue. Now that you have discovered it, I can do nothing but confess my crime!"

After hearing Wu Liang out, Lord Bao took an ink marker and showed it to him. "This was found in the temple. Look at it carefully: Is it yours?"

"I don't have to look at it," said Wu Liang with a sigh. "I dropped my ink marker when I took out my axe."

The murder case was thus settled. Wu Liang was made to sign his confession and taken to prison, where he would wait for his sentence.

Shen Qing was then brought into the hall, cleared of the murder charge, and awarded 10 taels of silver from the county treasury to compensate for his suffering a false charge. The Buddhist statue was carried back to the temple.

The crowd of people outside the *yamen* stared at the statue in wonder, and then gradually scattered.

Misadventures of a Fan Pendant

After Lord Bao solved that murder case by interrogating the Buddhist statue, the common people of Dingyuan County began to regard him as an upright official capable of telling right from wrong and ready to redress any injustice. Many came to the *yamen* to lodge their suits.

One day the big drum in front of the hall was being sounded. This meant someone had come to complain of an injustice.

Lord Bao had the man brought into the hall.

Two men, however, were brought in. One was in his twenties, and the other looked around 40 years old. The young man kneeled and spoke first.

"Your Excellency, your humble subject is named Kuang Bizheng. My uncle Kuang Tianyou runs a silk shop in this county. He has a coral fan pendant, which weights one *liang* (1 *liang*=1/20 kilogram) eight *qian* (1 *qian*=1/200 kilogram). He treasured the pendant very much, but unfortunately lost it three years ago. I used to play with the pendant a lot at my uncle's and knew it very well. While I was walking in the street today I saw the pendant dangling on this man's belt. I was not absolutely sure that the pendant was indeed the one my uncle had lost, so I asked very politely if I could take a look at it. But this man not only refused but began to curse me and call me a robber. That's why he grabbed me and brought me here. Please find out the truth about this, Your Excellency!"

After hearing the young man out, Lord Bao turned to

the other man, who said hastily in a strong southern accent, "I am a native of Jiangsu Province; my family name is Lü and my given name Pei. I came across this young lad today, and he just seized me and claimed the coral pendant I was carrying to be his. What a horrible man is this, trying to rob me in broad daylight! Please Your Excellency, find out the truth about this!"

After both men had finished speaking, Lord Bao had Lü Pei's pendant brought to him and examined it. Made of genuine light red coral, it had a glossy and smooth surface and looked quite nice.

Lord Bao weighed the pendant in his hand. "Kuang Bizheng, how much did you say this pendant weighs?"

"My uncle's pendant weighs one *liang* eight *qian*. It is possible that this pendant is not the one my uncle lost but only appears similar. But then it would surely be of a different weight. In that case I would certainly not claim it."

Lord Bao turned to ask Lü Pei, "Do you know how much this pendant weighs?"

"It is a gift from a good friend of mine," replied Lü Pei. "I have no idea how much it weighs exactly."

At this, Lord Bao told Bao Xing to bring a scale to weigh the pendant. It was exactly one *liang* eight *qian*. "Lü Pei," said Lord Bao, "the weight of this pendant is exactly as he said, so this must be the same one his uncle lost."

On hearing this, Lü Pei grew very anxious. "Oh, Your Excellency! This pendant is really a gift from a good friend! And why should I know its weight? We Jiangsu people don't know how to lie!"

"Your friend who gave this to you as a gift, what's his name?"

"His name is Pi Xiong. He is the leader of the horse peddlers and is quite well known in this area."

Lord Bao fell silent on hearing Pi Xiong's name. After a while he ordered Kuang and Lü to be taken away and sent some runners to bring Pi Xiong to the *yamen*. After that, he retreated to his room to have his meal.

Lord Bao did not speak while eating. When he was almost finished, he suddenly said to Bao Xing, who was standing beside him, "Do you remember the meal we had at an inn the first day we arrived in Dingyuan?"

"Yes, master!"

"When a man sat down at the table next to ours, the waiter brought him two wine pots and two cups. But he suddenly changed countenance and left in a hurry, without eating anything. Do you remember that?"

"Yes, I remember it very clearly, master!"

"Well, we will soon find out what lies behind all this!"

A runner came in to report that Pi Xiong had come. Lord Bao took his seat and ordered Pi Xiong to be brought into the hall. Pi kneeled in salute and said, "Your Excellency, why do you send for your humble subject?"

"I've heard that you have a coral fan pendant. Is that true?"

"Yes, I came by it three years ago."

"Have you given it to someone else?"

"No, I haven't," replied Pi Xiong. "I don't know who its owner is; how could I have given it to someone else!"

Lord Bao nodded. "Where is it then?"

"I keep it in my house."

Lord Bao beckoned Pi Xiong to be taken aside and ordered the runners to bring in Lü Pei. At the sight of Pi Xiong, Lü Pei had an uneasy look on his face. "Lü Pei," Lord Bao said, "Pi Xiong has just told me that he didn't give the pendant to you. How did you obtain it then? Speak!"

When Lü Pei replied hastily that the pendant was a gift from Pi Xiong's wife, Liu Shi, Lord Bao realized at once that there was a lot behind all this. "Why did Liu Shi give the pendant to you?"

Lü Pei turned red in the face but did not utter a word. Irritated, Lord Bao ordered the runners to slap him. Lü Pei waved his hands wildly when the runners were walking to him, saying, "Oh, Your Excellency, don't be angry with me! I'll tell the truth!" Thus he admitted to an illicit affair with Liu Shi, who had given the pendant to him as a love token.

Pi Xiong had a funny look on his face, listening to Lü Pei's account of his wife's infidelity. Lord Bao then ordered Liu Shi to be brought in. When questioned, Liu Shi had no difficulty at all recounting her affair with Lü Pei, for she had long cherished a grudge against her husband for keeping a lover. "My husband, Pi Xiong, has long been associated with Bi Shi, Yang Dacheng's wife. One day he returned from her residence with this pendant and told me to keep it for him. As I was friendly with Lü Pei, I gave the pendant to him as a gift."

On hearing this, Bao Xing thought to himself, "No wonder Lü Pei said the pendant was a gift from a 'good friend.' A good friend indeed!"

Lord Bao immediately issued an order to summon Bi Shi. Just then someone was heard beating the drum outside. Lord Bao had Lü, Pi, and Liu taken aside and the drummer brought in.

This man, about 50, turned out to be Kuang Bizheng's uncle, Kuang Tianyou. Hearing that his nephew had gotten into trouble because of the fan pendant, he hurried over to the *yamen* to bear witness for his nephew. "This pendant used to be mine," he said. "One day about three years ago, I asked Yang Dacheng to go to the silk shop with this pendant to fetch some silk with it. This pendant was known to all the silk shops in the county, so I found it convenient to use it as collateral to buy goods. When Yang failed to return with the silk a few days later, I went to ask about it at the silk shop, where I was told that Yang had never been there. So I hurried to Yang's home, where I learned that he had died the night of the very day I gave him the pendant. No one knew where the pendant had gone, and I had no choice but to accept it as a piece of bad luck. Today, however, my nephew saw the pendant on that man. Please, Your Excellency, find out the truth about this!"

After hearing him out, Lord Bao had Kuang Tianyou taken away. Bi Shi was brought in.

Bi Shi appeared to be in her early thirties and looked very attractive with her pretty face and nice figure. Almost three years after her husband's death, she was still dressed in mourning. However, there were traces of make-up on her face. When she entered the hall, there was a voluptuous sway to her walk. At the sight of her, Lord Bao became assured in his suspicion.

"What illness did your husband die of?" asked Lord Bao. "To answer the question of Your Excellency, he died of severe heart pain."

"But Kuang Tianyou said your husband was still working for him on the day he died."

"Your Excellency, my husband was seized by the illness suddenly. It was totally unexpected." She began to sob. "He has been dead for nearly three years. Why do you ask about him, Your Excellency? Is there a special reason for all this?"

Lord Bao smiled coldly. "Yes, there is! I already know the answer to my question; I asked you because I was curious to see how you would lie to me. Since you ask for the reason, I will tell you. Pi Xiong has just confessed to

19

me that you murdered your husband. Now what do you have to say?"

Bi Shi's face turned pale, then crimson, her eyebrows rising with indignation. "What? How dare he blame everything on me? Oh Your Excellency, it was Pi Xiong who murdered my husband!"

Not waiting to hear more, Lord Bao raised his hand and ordered, "Bring Pi Xiong here!"

At the sight of Bi Shi, Pi Xiong was quite alarmed. Lord Bao banged the table with his wooden block. "Pi Xiong, Bi Shi has confessed that you murdered her husband because of your illicit affair with her. What do you have to say?"

Seeing the indignant look on Bi Shi's face, Pi Xiong realized what had happened and lamented to himself, "What a stupid woman! You've been fooled without knowing it!" However, he was not ready to admit his guilt. "Your Excellency," he said, "it is true that Bi Shi and I have been rather friendly, but I didn't murder Yang Dacheng. Please find out the truth about this!"

Lord Bao could no longer suppress his anger. "You glib-tongued ruffian! Since you murdered Yang Dacheng, his ghost has been following you all along. Could you have forgotten how his ghost turned up behind you at the inn? You were so scared that you left without eating anything!"

Pi Xiong was flabbergasted. After the incident at the inn the waiter's words kept ringing in his ears. He was now convinced that Yang's ghost had been trailing him, and there was no escape. Half dazed, he muttered to himself, "Well, well, I'd better tell everything!" Thus he recounted how he struck up a relationship with Bi Shi. They became enamored with each other and, for fear of being discovered by Yang Dacheng, decided to get rid of him. They got him drunk, then killed him and hastily buried him, claiming that he had died of a sudden heart attack. Pi Xiong took the fan pendant and gave it to his wife, Liu Shi.

Lü Pei was dumbfounded as he listened to the unusual events surrounding the fan pendant that finally fell into his hands. Then Lord Bao announced his verdict. Pi Xiong and Bi Shi were thrown into prison, to be executed in autumn; Liu Shi would be sold as a servant, with the proceeds going into the county treasury; Lü Pei received 40 strokes of the birch amid loud cries of pain. As for the fan pendant, it was returned to Kuang Tianyou, its diligent, law-abiding, and lawful owner.

The Ghost
in the Crock

In the southeast of Dingyuan County lay a small village called Xiaoshawo, "Little Sand Dunes," which had dense woods in the hills but little arable land. Most villagers made a living by collecting and selling firewood. Among them was an old man named Zhang San, well known for his honesty and obstinance. He was always ready to help others even if it would bring harm to himself. So he became known by the nickname Zhang Biegu, "the eccentric and foolish Zhang."

Zhang San never married. He was over 60 and lived alone in a thatched house. He used to go into the hill to collect firewood, but now that he was too old for such heavy labor the villagers asked him to keep watch over and weigh the firewood they collected, and he was paid when the firewood was sold. They were willing to do this because he had helped others all his life.

One day there was not much work to do. It suddenly occurred to Zhang San that Zhao Da from Dongtawan still owed him over four hundred coins, the price of two loads of firewood. "Even though my fellow villagers do not suspect me of pocketing the money," he said to himself, "I owe it to them to get the money back. There's nothing else for me to do today, so I will go and collect that money."

So he took his walking stick, locked the door, and set out for Dongtawan.

When he came to Zhao Da's place, he was surprised to see a big, new house that could only belong to a very rich

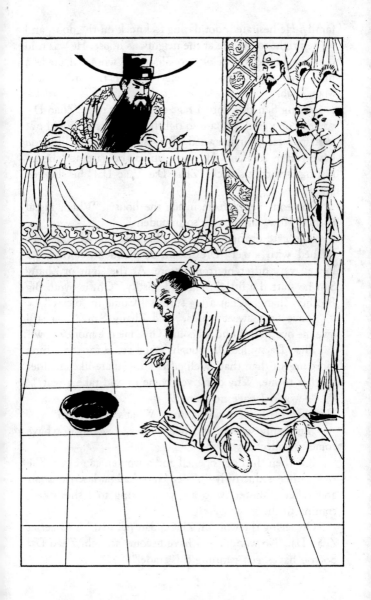

family. He hesitated, not daring to knock on the door, and turned right to inquire at the neighbor's house. He was told that the house did belong to Zhao Da, who had made a huge fortune and was now referred to in the area as Big Man Zhao.

Zhang San flew into a rage on hearing this. "Zhao Da, you son of a gun! You are so tightfisted that you would not even pay for your firewood. Why should a man like you have gotten so rich?" He went up to the gate and began hitting it with his stick. "Zhao Da! Zhao Da!" he shouted loudly.

Someone yelled from inside the house, "Which rascal is that? How dare you be so impudent!"

The gate opened to reveal Zhao Da himself, his face flushed with anger. Dressed·in resplendent clothes, he looked very different from before. At the sight of Zhang San he started a little, then said hastily, "Oh, it's you, Big Brother Zhang! What a big surprise! Come in, please!"

"Save your sweet words," said Zhang San. "You still owe me over four hundred coins. Give me the money now!"

Zhao Da smiled. "I thought you'd come for something more urgent than that! Well, after all, you are like an elder brother to me. Why don't you come in and take a seat?"

"I won't. I have no money."

Zhao Da burst out laughing. "What's this about?"

"I'm being serious. If I had money, I would not have come to collect my debt."

Just then the door opened and a woman came out. She was rather seductively dressed and had a lascivious air about her. "Master, who are you talking to?" she asked, coming to the gate.

On seeing the woman, Zhang San pointed his finger at Zhao Da. "No wonder you have become so rich, Zhao Da! So you have been running this trade!"

"Don't talk nonsense!" said Zhao Da. "This is your sister-in-law!" He turned to the woman. "It's no stranger. This is Elder Brother Zhang."

The woman came up and greeted Zhang San.

"Pardon me for not returning your greeting," said Zhang San. "I am suffering from a backache."

"You are still fond of joking," said Zhao Da with a smile. "Please come in."

With much reluctance Zhang San followed him into the house, where he saw many crocks piled on the ground. After they had taken their seats as host and guest, Zhao bade his wife pour tea. Zhang San waved his hand. "I don't drink tea. You owe me over four hundred coins and had better pay me. There's no need to play any trick."

"You don't need to worry, Elder Brother Zhang!" said Zhao Da. "How can I refuse to pay you the four hundred coins!" He told his wife to take out four hundred coins and give them to Zhang San. Zhang San put the coins in his inside pocket and stood up. "It's not that I want to make small gains," he said, "but as an old man I often have to get up to relieve myself at night. You have so many crocks here. Why don't you let me take one home to make up for the change you owe me? After that we will be even, and the next time we meet we won't need to greet each other."

"You are as bullheaded and caustic as ever!" said Zhao Da. "All these crocks have been carefully picked and have no holes in them. You may take any that you like."

At this Zhang San picked up a crock, held it to his chest, and turned to leave, without even stopping to say good-bye.

It was three *li* (one *li*=1/2 kilometer) from Dongtawan to the village. The withered trees and fallen leaves were caught in the evening glow. A cool autumn breeze was blowing in the woods. Walking with his stick, Zhang San fell into a bad mood. The more he thought about what he had seen the more indignant he grew. He simply could not understand why a man like Zhao Da could have grown so rich in just a few years.

A whirlwind swept across the ground, raising dust and leaves and tossing them against Zhang San's face. He shuddered and shrank with cold, holding his shoulders with both hands. The crock he had been carrying dropped to the ground and rolled a few turns before it stopped. A rueful voice seemed to be coming from inside it. "Ow! My waist hurts from the fall!"

Zhang San turned pale, thinking he must have run into an unhappy ghost in the forest. He spat on the ground, picked up the crock, and started to run. But he was too old to move very fast. A voice was crying behind him, "Uncle, wait for me!"

He turned to look but saw no one. Terrified, he started running again. "When a man has bad luck, even ghosts will make fun of him! I have never done anything wrong all my life, so why should I run into a ghost during the day? My days must be numbered!"

He staggered into his thatched cottage and, putting down the crock and his stick, locked the door and blocked it with a wooden chair. Then he stood there, gasping for breath.

Because of the running he felt weak all over and sat down on his bed, trying to take a rest. "What a ghost!" he muttered. "Let's see if you can get into my cottage to haunt me!"

No sooner had he spoken these words than he heard the woeful voice again. "Uncle, what a cruel death I died!"

Zhang San leaped from his bed in amazement. The voice had come from somewhere inside the room! He looked around. "Who are you? Where are you hiding?

What do you want?"

"Uncle, don't be afraid. I am in the crock you've brought home."

Hearing this, Zhang San turned to look at the crock but could see nothing inside it. But he was no longer afraid, now that he knew where the ghost was. "Who are you?" he asked again. "And what do you want of me?"

After a pause, the rueful voice replied, "My family name is Liu, and my given name Shichang. I lived in Babao Township outside the Changmen gate of Suzhou, with my mother, Zhou Shi, my wife, Wang Shi, and my three-year-old son, whose pet name was Baisui. I was a silk merchant. After finishing my business in Dingyuan, I hired a mule to carry my luggage and set out on my way back. That evening I was put up by Zhao Da, whom I took for a kindhearted host. But Zhao Da and his wife turned out to be so cold-blooded! When they learned that I was a merchant on my way home, and when they saw the heavy luggage I was carrying, they decided to kill me and rob me of my money. So they murdered me in the dead of night and, to remove all traces of their crime, they chopped my body into pieces, which they mixed with mud and baked into crocks. Thus I died a cruel death in a strange land. My mother, wife and son are still waiting for me to come home. Even as a ghost I can have no rest underground, and I ask you to forgive me for scaring you! I also want you to bring the case to Lord Bao, so that my murderers can be punished for their heinous crime and my ghost can rest in peace in the netherworld. If you will do all this for me, in my next life I will turn into a horse or a dog to repay your kindness!" The ghost began to weep bitterly.

The sad story made Zhang San's blood boil. He had always been ready to take up the cudgels against injustice done to anyone—even if the victim had become a ghost.

Now he was not in the least afraid. "Crock!" he shouted.

"Yes, Uncle!"

"I'll go to the *yamen* to demand justice for you! But there is one problem. Lord Bao will not believe me if I just tell him the story all by myself, without any evidence. You must come with me and bear out my testimony."

"Thank you so much, Uncle!" said the ghost. "I will go with you."

Zhang San was quite impressed by the clear voice of the ghost. "What a tenacious ghost he is!" he thought to himself. "So this was how Zhao Da got rich overnight—by murdering people for money! I am determined to help this ghost! If I take the talking crock with me, I shall have no difficulty convincing Lord Bao. On the other hand, I am an old man with a very bad memory. I have to memorize the ghost's name and address before I go to the *yamen*." So he ran over the story of the ghost in his mind several times until he knew it by heart, then went to bed. But he was too agitated to fall asleep. After a restless night, he got up before dawn and, picking up the crock and his walking stick, set out straight for the county *yamen*.

When he arrived at the county seat it was still very early and the city gate was not yet open. The early morning breeze in late autumn was very cold, sending shivers down his spine. He found shelter behind a rock, where he sat down to regain his breath. After a while he felt warm and his spirits rose. He placed the crock on the ground and began to sing a favorite tune, beating the crock with his stick to keep rhythm: "On the fifteenth day of the eighth month, in mid-autumn festival, the moon comes out to shine on my windowsill...." Just then he heard the city gate swing open with a loud screeching noise. Picking up the crock, he hurried into the city and went to the *yamen*, where Lord Bao was already sitting in the main hall ready to hear complaints. With loud cries of "injustice!" Zhang San was escorted by the runners into the hall and brought before Lord Bao.

Lord Bao looked down from his seat, finding an old, very thin man with an animated face. "Old man, what injustice have you suffered?" he asked.

Putting down the crock, Zhang San fell to his knees and began to recount his tale. "Your Excellency, it is the ghost in this crock who has suffered an injustice! I come here only to help him. Yesterday I went to collect a debt at Zhao Da's house, where I picked up this crock and took it home. Then I discovered that an unlucky ghost had attached himself to the crock. It was this ghost who told me how he had been murdered and begged me to sue his murderers on his behalf. If you don't believe me, Your Excellency, just ask this crock."

Astonished, Lord Bao did not know what to think of this. "Crock!" he shouted. There was no answer. Lord Bao shouted again and again, but not the slightest sound came from the crock. At this Lord Bao glanced at Zhang San and thought to himself, "What a befuddled old man!" He did not become angry, but simply said to the runners, "Take him out of here!"

Embarrassed, Zhang San picked up the crock and left. As soon as he was out of the *yamen*, he shouted to the crock, "Crock!"

"I am here, Uncle!" came the answer in a clear voice.

"What trick are you playing?" demanded Zhang San with great annoyance. "You begged me to cry injustice on your behalf at the *yamen*, but when Magistrate Bao called you, you never answered him! Why?"

"Uncle, I was not able to enter the *yamen*."

"Why not?"

"There is a god guarding the front gate, and ghosts

cannot enter. Please, Uncle, explain this to the Magistrate."

Hearing this, Zhang San walked back to the *yamen*. "Injustice!" he cried.

The runner on duty came over and recognized him. "Why don't you leave, you foolish old man? What are you crying about now?"

"Please tell this to the Magistrate," said Zhang San. "The ghost told me that he was stopped by the gate-god and could not enter the hall."

The runner reluctantly went in to report to Lord Bao. As soon as he heard this, Lord Bao picked up his writing brush and wrote a note: "The gate-god is not to stop the ghost from entering the hall to make complaints." He told the runner to burn the note before the gate and brought in the old man.

Zhang San entered the hall the second time. Putting down the crock, he again fell to his knees.

"When I call him this time, will the ghost answer me?" asked Lord Bao.

"Yes, Your Excellency," replied Zhang San.

"Listen carefully," said Lord Bao to the runners standing on both sides. Then he cried in a loud voice, "Crock!"

When there was no answer, Lord Bao shouted again. "Crock! Crock!"

There was still no answer.

Lord Bao flew into a rage. Banging the table with his wooden block, he shouted, "You old scoundrel! Because of your old age, I did not punish you the first time. How dare you come again to disrupt the court! Do you think you can fool me with your petty tricks?" He took a bamboo slip from the pot on his table and threw it to the ground. Getting the signal, the runners swarmed over to Zhang San, pushed him onto the ground and gave him 10 strokes of the birch. Zhang San screamed and wailed in pain.

When the beating was finished, Lord Bao said, "I only gave you 10 strokes because you are, after all, an old man. This should be enough to warn you against committing the same mistake again. Get out of here!"

Zhang San struggled to his feet, his buttocks swollen from the beating and his face crimson with shame and rage. Picking up his stick, he went limping to the gate. "Take your chamber pot with you!" shouted a runner behind his back. Zhang San turned back, picked up the crock, and went out. Some of the runners burst out laughing.

Coming out of the *yamen*, Zhang San threw the crock to the ground and turned to leave. "Ow! I've sprained my ankle!" A voice came from inside the crock.

At these words Zhang San was infuriated. He turned abruptly to the crock. "What? You have sprained your ankle? Look at what you've done to me! What on earth do you want to do? Poking fun at an old man? You think you can get away with all this?" He lifted his foot and was about to bring it down on the crock when the ghost cried in a woeful voice, "Take pity on me, Uncle! Take pity on a ghost unable to demand justice for himself!"

"Unable to demand justice for yourself? Why didn't you do it just now? I suffered such humiliation at the court, in front of the Magistrate, and you never uttered a single word! I am the one who is unable to demand justice!"

"Uncle, please forgive me for getting you into trouble. But I was really unable to enter the hall!"

"Why? Did the gate god still forbid you to go in?"

"It was not that, Uncle. Because I am naked, I can not meet a high official face to face. You have to cover me up. Please explain this to the Magistrate!"

"Thanks to you. I've already received 10 strokes of the birch," complained Zhang San. "Do you think I would walk

31

out of the *yamen* alive this time?" Nevertheless, he bent down to pick up the crock and walked back to the *yamen*. Because he was driven out of the hall a moment before, he dared not shout injustice at the gate. Instead, he slipped in through the side door. Two cooks caught sight of him. "Hey, Chief Hu! That old man has come again!" The runner named Hu was telling his companions about the funny old man when he heard the call. He came running over and caught hold of Zhang San, intending to make fun of him. However, Zhang San had his own way of dealing with this. He slumped to the ground and began shouting injustice at the top of his lungs.

"Who is making such a noise over there?" demanded Lord Bao. "Bring him here!"

Zhang San entered the hall for the third time. "What? It's you again!" said Lord Bao. "You still haven't had enough beating, foolish old man?"

Red-faced, Zhang San kneeled and kowtowed. "Your Excellency, when I walked out of the *yamen* and blamed the crock for failing to speak, he said he could not meet you because he was naked. If you could give him a piece of clothing, he will be able come in and answer your questions."

Lord Bao thought for a while, then told Bao Xing to bring a shirt and give it to Zhang San. Zhang San went out and covered up the crock with the shirt. "Crock, follow me into the court!" he said. A voice from inside the crock answered him, "Yes, Uncle!"

Zhang San went limping into the hall and placed the crock on the ground, kneeling beside it.

Lord Bao said to the runners, "Stand to attention, all of you, and listen carefully!" The runners forced back their snickers and put on a serious expression, all fixing their gaze on the ground.

"Crock!" shouted Lord Bao.

"Yes, Your Excellency!" A voice came from under the shirt.

Everyone in the hall was amazed to hear the voice except Zhang San, who leaped with joy. Only at the intimidating shout of the runners did he calm down, and fell to his knees again.

"Crock," said Lord Bao, "What injustice have you suffered? Tell me about it!"

"Your Excellency, I have told the whole story to Uncle Zhang," replied the voice from the crock, "and asked him to sue my murderers on my behalf."

Zhang San then answered Lord Bao's inquires in detail, recounting who the ghost was, where he had come from, and how he had been murdered by Zhao Da and his wife. The runners opened their eyes wide in disbelief.

When he had heard the story, Lord Bao bade Bao Xing bring 10 taels of silver, which he gave to Zhang San as a reward. Zhang was escorted home by a runner and told to make ready to be summoned as a witness.

Lord Bao had a letter written and sent to Suzhou, summoning the family members of the deceased to come to Dingyuan. In the meantime he sent runners to seize Zhao Da and his wife and bring them to the court.

When Zhao Da and his wife were interrogated, neither of them pleaded guilty. For lack of hard evidence no progress could be made.

Lord Bao thought for a while and ordered the two to be taken away. "Let them stay in separate cells," he told the runners, "and do not allow them to meet."

The following day Lord Bao ordered Zhao Da's wife, Diao Shi, to be brought into the hall. When she arrived, Lord Bao said to her, "Your husband has confessed. He said it was your idea to murder Liu Shichang, the merchant

33

from Suzhou. What do you have to say?"

Hearing that her husband had placed all the blame on her, Diao Shi flew into a rage and blurted everything out. She described how Zhao Da had killed Liu by strangling him with a rope, got rid of his body, and taken his money. She also said there were still over two hundred taels of silver left in their house. Lord Bao let her sign her confession and sent men to her house to bring back the silver.

Then Zhao Da was ushered into the hall. In spite of the evidence against him, Zhao Da still insisted he was innocent, claiming that the silver had been saved by him over many years. Enraged, Lord Bao ordered him to be taken to the rack and his feet placed in iron clamps. Even then Zhao Da refused to confess, so Lord Bao ordered the clamps to be tightened. Accustomed to a leisurely life and weak in physique, Zhao Da could not bear the torture and died on the spot.

According to law, severe torture like this could not be used arbitrarily. When it was needed, the Magistrate had to apply to his superiors for approval. Lord Bao used it against Zhao Da because he was furious. Seeing that Zhao was dead, he ordered the body to be carried away. Aware that he had made a grave mistake, he wrote a report to his superiors and waited for their response.

A few days later Liu Shichang's mother and wife arrived in Dingyuan, and what they said bore out Zhang San's words. Zhang San was then summoned to the court, where he retold the story about Liu Shichang's death. Lord Bao made the necessary arrangements for Liu's mother and wife, and had them escorted back to Suzhou. The case was thus settled.

Soon after, an order from the imperial court arrived stating that Lord Bao had broken the law by torturing a prisoner to death. However, as Zhao Da deserved a death sentence anyway, and as Lord Bao had always been a good official, he was exempted from prosecution. Instead, he was deprived of his post and demoted to commoner so that others would be warned against following his example.

Because of his outstanding talent, Lord Bao did not remain a commoner for long. A year later, he was reinstated as an official by the imperial court. Taking a lesson from Dingyuan, Lord Bao grew more cautious and attentive than before. By the time he died, he had become a high official respected all over the country for upholding justice on behalf of the common people.

As for the crock, after testifying in court, it no longer made any noise. Apparently the ghost, with his wrong redressed, could now rest in peace in the underworld. Zhang San took the crock home and buried it on a hill near the village. Around it he planted a few white birch trees, which grew to be very tall. In autumn, with their leaves fallen and branches dried up, many holes would emerge in their trunks, like big eyes staring out silently in the cold wind.

The Case of
the Woundless Corpse

Wang Bao, the Chief Minister, appreciated Lord Bao very much for his outstanding talents and recommended him repeatedly to the emperor. As a result, Lord Bao was appointed prefect of Kaifeng.

One day Lord Bao was sitting in the principal hall reading case files when someone cried injustice outside the gate. A villager in his fifties was brought in by the runners.

"What's your name, and what injustice have you suffered?" asked Lord Bao.

The man kneeled and kowtowed. "Your Excellency, my name is Zhang Zhiren, and I live in Qili Village in Xiangfu County. I had a cousin named Zhang Youdao, who lived only a few *li* from my home and made a living as a peddler. When I went to visit him a few days ago, his wife, Liu Shi, told me that he had been dead for three days. I asked her what illness killed him and why I had not been informed of his death. She replied that her husband had died of heart pain, and there had been no one in the house to send messages to the relatives. I became very suspicious about my cousin's sudden death, so I went to the *yamen* of Xiangfu County and demanded his coffin be unearthed and his body checked for wounds. The magistrate was kind enough to give his approval. When the coffin was dug up and opened, no wound or any other abnormality was found on the body. Liu Shi made quite a few nasty remarks about this, and the magistrate also got angry with me. He gave me 20 strokes of the birch, and I had to be bailed out by

my family. I stayed in bed for two days, but the more I thought about it the more suspicious I grew about my cousin's death. With nowhere else to go, I have come here to beg Your Excellency to listen to my complaint. Please find out the truth about this!"

"Was your cousin often ill?" asked Lord Bao.

"No, he wasn't."

"When was the last time you saw him alive?"

"I got along quite well with my cousin, and we paid each other frequent visits. He had called on me at home five days before I went to his house, where I was told that he had been dead for three days!"

On hearing this, Lord Bao thought to himself, "So Zhang Youdao died only two days after his cousin last saw him. Why should a perfectly healthy man have died so suddenly? Zhang Zhiren's suspicion is not entirely unfounded." He accepted Zhang Zhiren's complaint and ordered Liu Shi to be summoned to court.

Liu Shi was a woman around 25. Brought to the main hall of the *yamen*, she looked calm and not intimidated in the least. Instead, she muttered to herself in an indignant voice, "Why should a dead man be dug up and his body poked? What did he do in his lifetime to deserve such humiliation after his death? And what do they want with me here?" She did not peer in all directions nervously, but looked straight ahead and kneeled in salute to Lord Bao, as if accustomed to confronting others in court.

"Are you Zhang's wife, Liu Shi?" asked Lord Bao.

"I am Liu Shi, married to the peddler Zhang Youdao," replied the woman.

"What illness did your husband die of?"

"That evening my husband ate his supper and went to bed at the first watch. At the second watch, he suddenly said he felt pain in his heart. I was so scared. I got up and wanted to ask someone to find a doctor, but my husband began to cry out in great pain. A short moment later he was dead. Why should such misfortune have fallen on me!" She broke into tears.

Lord Bao banged the table with his wooden block. "Liu Shi, don't cover up the truth with your wily words! How did your husband die? You must tell the whole truth!"

Weeping bitterly, Liu Shi replied, "Your Excellency, I am filled with grief because of my husband's death. Why should I want to cover up anything?"

Lord Bao smiled coldly. "Liu Shi, Zhang Zhiren has already lodged his complaint with me about his cousin's sudden death. Now, let me ask you a question. If, as you said, your husband died of a sudden heart attack, why didn't you inform Zhang Zhiren? Why did you have your husband buried all by yourself?"

"Your Excellency, I have no one else to help me at home. Who could I find to send the message for me? What's more, I did not actually want to inform Zhang Zhiren."

"What do you mean by that?"

Liu Shi began to speak, then checked herself.

"Tell the truth!" cried Lord Bao. "Tell it quickly!"

"Yes, Your Excellency! But what a shame! When my husband was alive, Zhang Zhiren often found an excuse to come to our home. When my husband happened to be out, he would try to seduce me. I paid no attention to him, but when he discovered that I dared not mention this to my husband, he grew more and more unscrupulous. Not long ago, when he came to my house and learned of my husband's death, he showed no sign of grief but began to make shameful, disgusting remarks. I lost my temper and drove him away with loud curses. He became so angry with me because of this that he went to the *yamen* of Xiang-fu County and told the magistrate there was something strange about my husband's sudden death. He wanted to have my husband's coffin opened and his body examined. The magistrate granted his request ánd, when the coffin was opened and nothing unusual was found, gave him 20 strokes of the birch. However, Zhang is unwilling to give up, so he has come here to charge me. Why should my husband suffer such humiliation after his death? Why should my name be stained like this? I am terribly wronged and I beg Your Excellency to deal with the case justly!" With this she began to wail loudly.

Listening to her articulate and piteous account, Lord Bao thought to himself, "Zhang Zhiren has good reasons to be suspicious, but this woman's words are also hard to refute. There must be something behind all this. It's not a good idea to have the two confront each other in court. I have to do some investigating before going further." So he said to the woman, "According to what you just said, you have been wrongly accused. I will give Zhang Zhiren the punishment he deserves. You may go home now and wait for the court's summons in three days."

Retreating from the hall, Lord Bao bade Bao Xing prepare a small medicine chest, a signboard, and a set of clothes to go with them. He changed out of his official robe, slung the medicine chest over his back, and slipped out of the *yamen* through the side door, heading for Qili Village in Xiangfu County.

Qili (or "seven-*li*") Village was so named because it was only seven *li* from the prefecture seat. Arriving in the village, Lord Bao took out the signboard and began shaking a string of bells. As he walked, he chanted the following: "If you are ill, don't wait! To ignore an illness is like raising a tiger; once the tiger grows up it will devour you. Any strange and complicated cases will be eliminated through my hands. To the poor and needy, no prescription fee will be charged."

Shouting his way to the west end of the village, Lord Bao was stopped by an old woman. "Mister," she called out from a distance. "Come here please! Come here!"

Lord Bao went up to her. "Do you need any help?"

"Yes, please. Do you just sell pills, or do you also treat illnesses?"

"I sell pills and also treat illnesses. Why do you ask, grand auntie?"

"That's great!" said the old woman. "Mister, a few days ago some people came to the village shaking bells, but they only sold pills and could not treat illnesses. My daughter-in-law has been ill in bed for many days. Please come in and have a look at her."

Lord Bao was ushered into the house. This was a poor family having only three rooms with thatched roof, and the courtyard was stacked high with firewood and hay. Lifting a cloth curtain, the old woman invited Lord Bao to enter the west room and sit on the *kang* (a heatable brick bed). She took a small wooden bench and sat down beside him. "What's your honorable family name?" she asked.

"My name is Bao. What's yours, grand auntie?"

"So you are Doctor Bao. My husband's surname is You, but he died a long time ago. I have a son by the name of Gou'er. He works for Chen Yingjie, a big landlord living in the east end of the village. I have managed to find a wife for him. My daughter-in-law is a nice girl. She is more filial than my own son! But unluckily she has been ill for more than half a month. She is low-spirited, has no appetite, and often has fever in the afternoon. What is wrong with her, doctor? I am afraid you'll have to take the trouble to feel her pulse and prescribe some medicine for her."

"Where is she now?" asked Lord Bao.

"In the east room. I'll go and tell her."

The old woman turned and walked into the east room. Lord Bao overheard the following conversation:

"Good girl, I have found a doctor for you. You'll surely get well after he takes a look at you and prescribes some medicine."

"Oh mother, don't bother. It's nothing serious, and how are we going to pay him?"

"Didn't you hear what the doctor said just now? To ignore an illness is like raising a tiger. What's more, he will not charge us any prescription fee. Let's ask the doctor to look at you. It will save me from worrying every day if you get well. As you know, I have lost faith in my son. All I can depend on is you."

"All right mother," the daughter-in-law finally said. "Ask the doctor to come in."

"That's my good girl," the old woman said with delight. "What a filial daughter!" She came over and invited Lord Bao to enter the east room. The young woman was sitting on the *kang*, wrapped in an old quilt. Her face was clean and pretty, though sallow because of illness. Well versed in medicine, Lord Bao sat down by the *kang*, felt the woman's pulse for a while, then stood up and left the room. He and the old woman returned to the west room, where he told her, "Your daughter-in-law has a double pulse. She must be pregnant."

"Yes, she surely is! It must be four or five months old by now."

"In my opinion, her illness is due to blockage of vital energy caused by rage. Without timely treatment, it will probably develop into consumption. Grand auntie, you have to tell me what caused the illness before I can prescribe medicine for her properly."

"You are a living god!" exclaimed the old woman. "Her illness was surely caused by rage! Let me tell you everything from the beginning...."

"Mother, please don't!" came the young woman's weak voice from the east room. "Family troubles are unfit to be mentioned to strangers!"

"The doctor is no stranger," retorted the old woman. "He's going to save your life!" She turned to Lord Bao and continued, "My son works as a hired hand for the Chen family in the east of the village. His employer, Chen, is quite generous with my son, so we have always had enough to eat. When my son came home one day, he suddenly took out two silver ingots and placed them on the *kang*...."

"Mother, please don't continue!" said the young woman from the east room.

"My child, don't worry about anything," responded the old woman. "Just keep good care of yourself!" She went on, "I grew suspicious when I saw the ingots, so I insisted that he tell me everything. My son explained that Chen was having an affair with the wife of Zhang Youdao, a peddler from the neighboring village. A few days before, Chen had gone to Zhang's house to meet her but bumped into Zhang. So he planned to murder Zhang. He gave my son two silver ingots and...."

"Mother, please stop!" urged the young woman from the east room. "How can you mention this to others?"

The old woman got impatient. "My daughter, do you think I am telling this for my own amusement? I am trying to have you cured! The doctor must know the cause of the illness before he can treat you!"

"Yes!" agreed Lord Bao. "I won't know what medicine to prescribe until I learn what caused the illness."

The young woman fell silent, and the old woman went on with her story. "He gave my son two silver ingots and asked him to find something for him. My daughter-in-law tried to persuade my son not to get involved in Chen's plot. She pleaded with him on her knees, but my son refused to listen and kicked her. He picked up the ingots and left. Since then, he has stayed away from home. Later we learned of Zhang Youdao's sudden death. We also learned that when he was about to be buried, a loud noise came from his coffin as if his body were about to come back to life. Even the monks hired to handle the funeral became scared and ran away. Because of this, my daughter-in-law grew more and more worried each day, and this is how she got her illness."

After hearing her out, Lord Bao thought for a moment and wrote a prescription. Then he took a few pills from his medicine chest and handed them to the old woman.

"I have written for you an old, very effective recipe for protecting the fetus and improving blood circulation. You can let your daughter-in-law take these pills first. Remember, these should be taken with old wine."

The old woman thanked Lord Bao repeatedly. Lord Bao picked up his medicine chest and was ready to leave. "Your son did Chen a big favor," he said. "Hasn't Chen given your son something in return?"

"My son said Chen had promised him six *mu* (one *mu*=1/15 hectare) of land."

"Was he given a title deed to the land?"

"No! It was just an empty promise, I think."

"That is not fair!" exclaimed Lord Bao. "By doing him such a big favor, your son deserves to get sixty instead of six *mu* of land from Chen. A written statement is needed; otherwise Chen may go back on his word. Well, let me write a statement for you. If Chen goes back on his words, you can go to the *yamen* with this statement and demand the land." He wrote a statement on which he signed the name "Bao Qubing" and gave it to the old woman. She took it with great delight and bowed to him in gratitude.

Lord Bao flung the medicine chest on his back, tucked away his bells and signboard, and returned to his office in high spirits. "The case of Zhang Youdao is over," he thought to himself. "Now I can have You Gou'er arrested. Unfortunately, his wife will soon become a widow just like his mother, for he will undoubtedly be sentenced to death. On the other hand, I have done something for these two innocent women—six *mu* of land will help them get by."

On his return to Kaifeng Prefecture, Lord Bao immediately sent runners to arrest You Gou'er in secret. The following day, You Gou'er was found in a wineshop and taken to the *yamen*. Lord Bao immediately had him brought to the main hall for interrogation.

You Gou'er kneeled and kowtowed. Lord Bao asked, "Are you You Gou'er?"

"Your humble subject is rather named Lüzi."

"There is no doubt that you are Gou'er," said Lord Bao in a harsh voice. "Why do you call yourself Lüzi? Are you trying to make fun of your prefect?"

"To answer your question, Your Excellency, I dare not do that! I used to be called Gou'er, but someone told me Lüzi would be better, because a donkey is larger than a dog. Since you don't like it, Your Excellency, I can use my old name, Gou'er."

"Stop babbling nonsense!" shouted the runners.

"Gou'er!" Lord Bao called out again.

"Yes, I'm here!" answered Gou'er hastily. "It's true that a man's fate is predetermined," he muttered to himself. "I am not even allowed to change my name to make myself sound bigger."

Lord Bao said, "A ghost named Zhang Youdao has come to me to accuse Chen Yingjie and you of murdering him. As I see it, Chen was responsible for the murder, for he wanted to take Zhang's wife; you were not to blame although you received two silver ingots from him, because you could not disobey your employer. If you tell everything truthfully, I will make sure that you are not charged. So you don't need to worry, just tell me everything from the beginning."

Gou'er was terribly scared when he heard Zhang's ghost had accused him. When the silver ingots were mentioned, he became convinced that the prefect already knew everything. When told that he would not be charged for the crime, and on seeing Lord Bao's mild expression, he finally calmed down. Kowtowing to Lord Bao, he replied:

"Your Excellency, since you will be so kind as to spare me, I will tell the truth of the matter. This is how it all started: My employer was good friends with Zhang Youdao's wife, Liu Shi, but not with Zhang himself. One day he went to Zhang's house to meet Liu Shi, but Zhang bumped into them. He returned home and fell ill. He missed Liu Shi a lot, but dared not visit her again. Finally he decided he had better get Zhang Youdao out of the way. If Zhang were dead, it would be much easier for him to go and visit Liu Shi, or for her to come and visit him. So one day he sent for me and asked, 'Gou'er, my brother, can I ask you to do something for me?' I said, 'Master, you don't have to ask; just tell me what to do.' He said, 'This will not be easy. You have to look for it carefully.' I asked what unusual thing he wanted me to find. He said, 'I need you to find a rare insect called *shigui*. It's about the size of one's fingertip, and it has a golden head and a shining tail. It's really very hard to find.' When I asked where to look for it, he said, 'You must go to the graveyard. You will only find this insect in a tomb where the body has decayed but the brain has not dried up.' When I heard that, I could not make up my mind. But my employer took out two silver ingots and handed them to me. He said, 'You can take this. After you find the insect, I'll give you six *mu* of land. You must find it no matter how long it takes you. From now on you don't have to work during the day; just rest yourself so you have full strength to work at night.' Just as you said, Your Excellency, I could not disobey him. After that I went to the graveyard every night, and finally I found the *shigui*. Chen told me to dry it in the sun and grind it into fine powder. This powder is very poisonous. When mixed into food or tea, it will make a man die of heart pain and leave no trace except for a tiny red spot between his eyebrows. A few days later Zhang Youdao died; maybe this powder was put into his food. All this happened sometime ago. Please, Your Excellency, help me!"

Listening attentively, Lord Bao was convinced that Gou'er had told the truth. He took the written record of the confession, read it through, and had Gou'er sign it. "When Chen Yingjie is brought here later, you must confront him face to face. Only in this way can I help you get out of this trouble."

"I am so grateful, Your Excellency, for your great kindness," said Gou'er. "I am willing to confront Chen here." Lord Bao nodded and had Gou'er taken away. He then sent men to seize Chen Yingjie.

Soon after, Chen Yingjie was brought into the hall. Lord Bao went straight to the point. "Chen Yingjie, how did you murder Zhang Youdao? Confess all about your crime!"

Staggered, Chen Yingjie tried to deny everything. "No,

Your Excellency, I never did anything like that!"

Enraged, Lord Bao banged his wooden block on the table and said harshly, "You ruthless scoundrel, how dare you tell lies in front of your prefect! Runners, bring Gou'er!"

Gou'er came into the hall. At the sight of Chen Yingjie, he said, "Oh, you've come, master! Zhang Youdao's ghost has told the prefect what we did together. His Excellency already knows that I am not to blame because you ordered me to do it. It was your idea to begin with, and you gave me the silver—I didn't ask for it. Anyway, whatever you did, you can just confess to the prefect."

Chen Yingjie shuddered with fear at the very sight of Gou'er. After hearing these words, he was struck speechless. After a long pause, he said to Lord Bao, "I will answer Your Excellency's question truthfully. Your humble subject has indeed had an unlawful relationship with Liu Shi. As for murdering her husband, Zhang Youdao, there was nothing of the sort! I must have offended Gou'er somehow, so he is now trying to bring up a false charge against me. Don't be deceived by that ruffian, Your Excellency!"

Lord Bao realized that Chen was trying to evade the major charge by admitting a minor one. He said with a cold smile, "According to you, Gou'er has been lying to me? Well, take Gou'er out and beat him!"

Alarmed, Gou'er cried out, "Your Excellency! Every single word of mine is true! Let me ask him!" He turned to Chen Yingjie. "Master, didn't you ask me to look for an insect called *shigui*? If not, why should I have spent so much time digging in the graveyard every night? When I finally found one for you, you were not satisfied but said to me, 'How can such a small insect kill people? How can this be true!' You also told me to take it to Liu Shi and tell her, 'Don't pinch it in your hand; just wrap it in a piece of paper and pour it into food or tea.' Are these not your own words? How could I be lying? You also promised to give me six *mu* of land. Do you want to deny that too?" He turned to Lord Bao and kowtowed. "Your Excellency, instead of beating your humble subject, it's better to beat him. That will surely make him confess."

"All right," Lord Bao said with a smile. "I'll have him beaten. Runners, take Chen Yingjie out and give him 40 strokes of the birch!"

The runners responded with a thunderous roar and came over to grab Chen, who cried out, "No! Don't beat me! I will confess! I will confess!" He began to recount how he committed adultery with Liu Shi and plotted with her to murder Zhang Youdao. His confession bore out the testimony given by Gou'er earlier.

Just then a runner came in to report, "Liu Shi and You's mother and wife have come!" Lord Bao ordered Liu Shi to be brought in first.

Liu Shi walked into the hall, looking as composed as ever. At the sight of Chen Yingjie, however, she turned pale with fright.

Lord Bao did not speak to Liu Shi. "Chen Yingjie," he said, "tell what you did, in front of Liu Shi."

In a choking voice Chen said to Liu Shi, "We thought what we did would not be discovered, but Zhang Youdao's ghost has charged us to the prefect. Our deed is uncovered, and there is no use denying it. I have already signed my confession. You'd better also confess to save yourself from beating."

On hearing this, the woman began to curse in a loud voice. "You idiot! Why didn't I realize you are so stupid and worthless! Now that you have told everything, what can I do but do the same?"

Thus she also admitted to the crime. She also said the

charge against Zhang Zhiren of trying to seduce her was also false. Lord Bao had her sign her confession, then ordered the two women from the You family to be brought in.

You Gou'er's mother and wife came into the hall, both in tears. They failed to recognize Lord Bao sitting high above. Lord Bao asked, "You Gou'er told me Chen had promised him six *mu* of land. Is there a written statement?"

The old woman nodded. "At first there wasn't, but later I feared Chen would go back on his words, so I asked someone to write one for me. Here it is, Your Excellency. It bears the name of the guarantor and his signature." She took out a sheet of paper from inside her sleeve and handed it to Lord Bao. Lord Bao took the paper and could not help smiling when he read the deed he had written himself. Turning to Chen Yingjie, he said, "Since you have promised You Gou'er six *mu* of land, and there is a written contract about it, you should now give the land to him."

Preoccupied with the verdict awaiting him, Chen Yingjie nodded his headed repeatedly. Lord Bao wrote a note to Xiangfu County ordering the matter be done accordingly.

The case was about to close. Lord Bao asked Chen Yingjie, "Where did you learn about the poisonous quality of *shigui*?"

"The tutor in my house told me."

Lord Bao ordered the tutor to be brought in at once. The tutor was named Fei. Lord Bao asked, "Why should a person like you teach him how to use a deadly poison?"

Fei replied, "What I studied was Confucian doctrine, and that is also what I teach for a living. However, in my spare time I like to read medical books and came to know something about the use of drugs. On days when my employer stays home because of bad weather after I have finished teaching the children, I often chat with him and sometimes I would mention the function of drugs. I once said that drugs must be used with the greatest care because some are antagonistic to each other by nature, and I also mentioned a few poisonous things, such as *shigui*. It was just a casual remark on my part, and who could have known that he remembered what I told him and committed murder in such a manner! Please, Your Excellency, I have told the whole truth!"

"Though you did not teach him on purpose how to use poison," said Lord Bao, "as a Confucian scholar you should have known what was fit to speak about and what was not. Do you really think deadly poison a fit topic in casual conversation? I will mete out a light punishment for you, so that you won't commit the same mistake again!"

Thus Lord Bao had Fei expelled from Xiangfu and escorted to a remote place. Chen Yingjie and Liu Shi were to be beheaded at once. As for You Gou'er, he was sentenced to death and would be executed in autumn. Zhang Zhiren, the accuser, was sent away. With mixed feelings Lord Bao watched in silence as You Gou'er's mother and wife, supporting each other, walked out of the principal hall of the *yamen* of Kaifeng Prefecture.

Execution of
the Marquis of Anle

As prefect of Kaifeng, Lord Bao conducted trials of many complicated cases and soon became famous for unswervingly upholding the law and justice. A renowned scholar, Gongsun Ce, arrived to offer his service to Lord Bao and became a trusted advisor. One day Lord Bao was taking a rest in his house when Bao Xing entered to report that Wang Chao, Ma Han, Zhang Long, and Zhao Hu from Earth Dragon Hill in Shanxi Province were waiting outside the gate. Lord Bao had met them earlier when they were robbers based on the hill. Learning that Lord Bao had taken office in Kaifeng, they abandoned their fortress and came to offer their service to him.

Lord Bao hastily went out of the gate to meet the four ex-robbers, who saluted him respectfully. Zhao Hu, of a very impetuous disposition, was the first to throw himself on the ground. Lord Bao invited them into his studio and, after an exchange of greetings, they told Lord Bao that they had brought with them an old man they had rescued on their way, from the Tiexian Taoist Temple in Xiangfu County. The man, shut up by Taoist priests under a big bronze bell, had been on his way to the capital to lodge a complaint.

Hearing this, Lord Bao had the man brought into the studio.

The old man entered and kneeled before Lord Bao, tears rolling down his cheeks. "Your Excellency, what an injustice have I suffered!"

Lord Bao helped the old man onto his feet and bade him speak his grievance.

"My name is Tian Zhong," the old man said, "and I am a native of Chenzhou. Chenzhou had a crop failure this year, and the emperor was kind enough to send Pang Kun, the Marquis of Anle, to relieve the famine. However, since his arrival in Chenzhou the marquis has given no relief supplies to famine victims. Instead, he has built a magnificent private garden and seized many young women from local households. My master is named Tian Qiyuan, his wife Jin Yuxian, and they lived together with his aged mother. After the old lady recovered from an illness, Lady Jin went to the temple to offer thanks to the Buddha. Unfortunately, the marquis happened to be there. Attracted by her good looks, he had her snatched and taken away. When my master, Tian Qiyu, went to demand her release, the marquis had him arrested and thrown into prison. His mother was so terrified that she suffered a relapse of her chronic illness and died soon afterwards. I had the old lady buried and told myself that I must do something for my master and mistress. No one dared to touch the marquis in Chenzhou, so I decided to bring the case to the capital to demand justice. Not far from the capital I stayed the night at a Taoist temple, where I mentioned to the priests the purpose of my trip. However, the priests turned out to be cohorts of the marquis. They tied me up and placed me under a giant bronze bell. I would never see the light of day again but for the brave men here, who rescued me from the temple. With the help of Your Excellency, my master and mistress will not wait too long for justice to be restored! Thank heaven for being so merciful!"

The old man's voice turned hoarse with excitement. Lord Bao told Bao Xing to take the man away and put him up. Everything was done quietly so that people from the marquis's residence would not learn of it.

Lord Bao was fully aware of the power and prestige enjoyed by the Pang family in the imperial court. Pang Kun's father, Pang Ji, was none other than the chief minister and the emperor's father-in-law. That was why the marquis had always been able to commit outrageous crimes with impunity.

Furthermore, when Lord Bao took the civil recruitment examination many years before, Pang Ji happened to be the supervising official. As a result, Lord Bao had to acknowledge him as his master.

Lord Bao spent a restless night. He thought for a long time in his studio and finally composed a petition to the emperor.

The following morning Lord Bao entered the court and presented his petition to Emperor Renzong. In it he claimed that the wrong person had been placed in charge of relief work in Chenzhou. This resulted in widespread discontent among the local people and was a reflection on the honor and prestige of the imperial court. When the emperor looked displeased after reading the petition, Lord Bao went up to answer his inquires and mentioned briefly the injustice suffered by Tian Qiyuan. At this, Emperor Renzong fell silent. In spite of his forthrightness, Lord Bao was commendable for his loyalty, and malpractices obviously existed in the relief work in Chenzhou that needed to be thoroughly investigated. After careful consideration, Emperor Renzong conferred on Lord Bao the prestigious title "Grand Academician of the Dragon Diagram Hall" and charged him with investigation of the case in Chenzhou and of any case that might arise on the way.

Before coming to see the emperor, Lord Bao had prepared for the worst, fearing that the emperor might get so angry upon reading the petition as to strip him of his post or demote him. Delighted by the emperor's decision, he kneeled to express his gratitude, then asked for an additional favor. "With no symbol of authority in my hand, I fear that others may not obey me."

The emperor smiled. "All right, I will give you three imperial emblems, which will empower you as an imperial envoy. The design of the emblems is up to you. Think about this and report to me tomorrow."

Back in his residence, Lord Bao told his assistants what had happened during his audience with the emperor. When he mentioned the imperial emblems, he turned to Gongsun Ce. "Mr. Gongsun, please think carefully how we should design the three imperial emblems to make them most useful. I have to report to His Majesty tomorrow."

Gongsun Ce returned to his room and began racking his brains. With no clue from the emperor, the emblems had to be designed from scratch. They must symbolize imperial authority and accord with the emperor's wishes. Gongsun Ce thought so hard that he became dizzy. Grabbing a writing brush and a piece of paper, he scribbled a strawchopper, then added two more. He divided the choppers into high, medium, and low grades by the device of a dragon, a tiger, and a dog respectively. While he was gazing at his composition, Lord Bao entered the room. Gongsun Ce felt embarrassed when Lord Bao examined the picture carefully. To his surprise, Lord Bao banged the desk in excitement and exclaimed, "Excellent!" Smiling broadly, he said, "You are such a talented man! I admire you so much for your wonderful idea! The division into the three grades of dragon, tiger and dog is especially smart!"

Lord Bao sent for Bao Xing at once. "Find some blacksmiths and have them work overnight to make the molds for these choppers. I will have to show them to the emperor tomorrow morning." Turning to Gongsun Ce, he said, "Mr. Gongsun, you will take the trouble of giving instructions to the workmen. There is no need to report to me anymore."

Half in a daze, Gongsun Ce set down to work. He drew a more detailed diagram of the three choppers, marking out specifications and describing methods of mounting copper sheets and gold nails and attaching animal-heads. Soon the blacksmiths arrived. Guided by Gongsun Ce, they worked hectically all night and finished making the molds the following morning.

Lord Bao examined the molds carefully and had them placed into a yellow wooden box, which he took with him to the palace. After saluting the emperor, he said, "Your Majesty, in accordance with your edict yesterday endowing me with three imperial emblems, I have worked out the design. I dare not have them made without authorization and have therefore brought them here for inspection and approval."

With the emperor's assent, the yellow box was carried in and opened. The emperor looked down and saw the molds of three choppers decorated with dragon, tiger, and dog motifs. Each was a piece of superb workmanship.

"Whoever breaks the law," said Lord Bao, "will be executed with the chopper corresponding to his official rank."

Emperor Renzong realized what Lord Bao had in mind: To intimidate the unruly local officials with the three choppers. Much pleased, he approved Lord Bao's design of the imperial emblems and ordered them to be made at once. As soon as the choppers were ready, Lord Bao was to set out for Chenzhou.

At the sight of the chopper molds, some court officials began making comments to one another. Quite a few felt threatened and changed countenance.

From then on the three choppers became an indispensable part of Lord Bao's office, whereby he had the right to execute a high official without prior approval from the emperor. Because of this, he was able to uphold the law and redress the grievances of the common people against powerful evildoers.

Lord Bao kowtowed in gratitude to the emperor and left the court. On his way back to his office, his sedan chair was stopped by 10 old men kneeling on the road. Holding a written complaint, they uttered loud cries of "Injustice!" As Lord Bao had told the runners not to stop anyone from holding up his sedan chair and submitting their complaints, Bao Xing went over and took the written complaint, which he handed to Lord Bao. After a short moment Lord Bao lifted the curtain of his sedan chair, tore the paper into pieces, and threw them away. "What sheer nonsense!" he said harshly. "Tell the local constable to drive these ruffians out of the capital! Otherwise they will try to create trouble in front of other officials!" He ordered the sedan chair to be lifted again and continued on the way to his office.

The old men were staggered. When the local constable came to chase them away, they began to cry and wail. "We endured so many hardships traveling from Chenzhou to the capital because we thought Lord Bao would uphold justice. But he turns out to be just like all the other officials —they shield one another and give no thought to the common people! There is no hope of redressing the injustice we have suffered!" Then they burst into tears.

The local constable urged them to move, saying, "Go on, go on! Don't let me take the blame for you. It's no use crying. You are not the only ones to suffer an injustice!" The old men had no choice but to follow the constable, heading for the city gate.

When they were out of the city, a man on horseback caught up with them and said to the constable, "You have driven these people out of the city—that's all you need to do. Now you may go back." The constable turned and went back into the city.

The rider was Bao Xing. He trailed the old men until they came to a quiet place, then went up to them. "I work for Lord Bao of Kaifeng Prefecture," he announced. "It is not that my master doesn't want to hear your complaint. Just then there were too many people in the street, and it would be undesirable for others to learn of the case. My master told me to stop you from leaving. Soon he will set off on an inspection tour to Chenzhou. Now you should put up at some secluded place and, when Lord Bao leaves for Chenzhou, follow him there. Two of you may come back with me to the *yamen*; my master has some questions for you." The old men were filled with joy upon hearing this. Two of them followed Bao Xing to the *yamen* of Kaifeng.

Lord Bao bade the two old men explain the case in detail. It turned out that 13 families in all had fallen victim to the Marquis of Anle. Among those, the head of one family was dead, another was ill in bed, and still another was locked up in prison. So only 10 men had come to the capital. After hearing them out, Lord Bao admonished, "Don't tell this to anyone else. When I leave the capital, you must follow me quietly."

After Lord Bao received the emperor's approval to make the three choppers, Gongsun Ce lost no time supervising the work. A few days later, three deadly sharp and awesome-looking choppers were ready. Four brave men were put in charge of the choppers, with each assigned a specific duty: Zhang Long and Zhao Hu would carry in the criminal, Ma Han would tie him up, and Wang Chao would bring the chopper down.

When all was ready, Lord Bao left for Chenzhou with his retinue. Gongsun Ce took Tian Zhong with him, and the 10 old men from Chenzhou followed unobtrusively behind.

Pang Kun, the Marquis of Anle, regarded his relief mission to Chenzhou as a grand opportunity to enjoy himself. Relying on his father's clout, he was able to gather many followers, and he had set out for Chenzhou in their company. He did not provide any relief supplies to the people; instead, he conscripted many able-bodied men from local households to build a magnificent garden. He also abducted a lot of young women in Chenzhou, taking the pretty ones as his temporary concubines, and the rest he used as maid-servants. The officials of Chenzhou, including the governor himself, vied with one another to curry his favor. The people of Chenzhou were unfortunate enough to suffer a severe crop failure that year, but the arrival of the marquis made life even more difficult for them. Many were even forced to leave their homes.

After abducting Jin Yuxian, Pang Kun had her locked up in the Lifang Building in his garden. He tried every means to bring her to submission, but in vain. Born into a wealthy family and properly brought up, Jin Yuxian was prepared to die to protect her chastity. Enamored with her good looks, Pang Kun was at first unwilling to use force against her. So he resorted to his concubines, who were sent to persuade Jin to follow their example and enjoy herself. Filled with indignation, Jin Yuxian upbraided the concubines for their shamelessness. Just then Pang Kun came up the stairs led by two maid-servants. "You needn't try to persuade her," he said with a smile. "Since this beauty is unwilling, I will not compel her." He turned to Jin. "Here is a cup of warm wine to bid you farewell. After you drink it up, I'll have you escorted back to your home tomorrow morning." Actually, an aphrodisiac had been mixed into the wine to trick Jin Yuxian into submission. When he took the cup and presented it to Jin Yuxian, she hastily swept it to the floor to prevent him from getting too close to her. Furious, Pang Kun shouted, "What a shrew! What a dreadful woman!" He ordered Jin to be tied up, intending to take her by force. Just then someone was heard rushing up the steps. A maid-servant came in and reported, "Your Highness, the governor wants to see you about something very urgent. He is waiting in the hall."

Pang Kun knew the governor would not have called on him at night but for something really pressing. He said to his concubines, "Try to talk some reason into this silly woman! Let's see what else she is capable of doing!"

He went across the building and entered the hall. The governor, Jiang Wan, rose to greet him. Pang Kun took the seat of honor as the host and Jiang Wan sat down opposite him. Pang Kun asked, "You must have something important to tell me by your night visit."

"Your Highness, I have just received a circular from the imperial court notifying me that His Majesty has sent Bao Zheng, the Grand Academician of the Dragon Diagram Hall, to investigate your relief mission in Chenzhou. He will arrive in five days. The news has made me very worried. I have come to inform you of this, so we can see what we can do about it."

Pang Kun did not feel perturbed. "Black-faced Bao is a disciple of my father's," he said. "He will be sensible enough not to find fault with me."

"With respects," said Jiang Wan, "Your Highness is mistaken. According to my information, this black-faced

Bao shows partiality to no one. What's more, on this trip he has brought with him the three execution choppers recently given to him by the emperor. With these choppers he has the right to execute any official without asking prior permission of the court. We should be careful!" He moved close to Pang Kun and whispered, "Do you think Bao can be ignorant of what you've done in Chenzhou?"

Pang Kun began to grow a little fearful, but he still tried to brush it aside. "Even if he knows everything, what can he possibly do against me, the Marquis of Anle?"

"No, you don't understand!" the governor got very agitated. "As I have found out, these imperial choppers fall into three classes—the dragon chopper, the tiger chopper and the dog chopper. When someone has committed a capital offense, even if he belongs to the imperial family, Bao has the right to behead him first and report to the court afterward. You must not take this too lightly!"

Pang Kun was struck speechless. After a long pause he said, "Well, what shall we do?"

"Your Highness, I have come here tonight to discuss this problem. Up to now I have not come up with a good solution. Everything would be fine if black-faced Bao were dead. But how could we make that happen?"

Something occurred to the marquis upon hearing this. "I have an idea!" he exclaimed, rolling his eyes. "I have someone equal to the task." He turned and shouted to a steward outside the door, "Pang Fu, go and bring Xiang Fu here at once!"

"I have a very brave man named Xiang Fu," he explained to Jiang Wan. "He has learned superb martial arts skills from a great master and can leap onto roofs and over walls without difficulty. He came to join my following not long ago. I can send him to intercept black-faced Bao on the way and get rid of him then and there. Won't that be nice?"

"Good! Let's do it!" said the governor. "But does the man have enough courage to do the job?"

"Wait till I ask him."

A short moment later Pang Fu, the steward, returned with another man, who was very tall and strongly built, his face covered in whiskers. His very presence was imposing and fearsome. He saluted Pang Kun and was introduced to the governor. He turned to salute the governor, who took him by the hands, saying, "No need to stand on ceremony, brave man!"

"This is indeed a very brave man," he said to Pang Kun with a smile. "He will no doubt carry out our plan successfully! But I wonder if he is willing to do his best?"

Pang Kun burst into laughter. "You don't need to worry about that, Mr. Jiang. I have full confidence in his courage. He won't cower before this!"

Not knowing what they were referring to, Xiang Fu asked, "Your Highness, what do you want me to do?"

Pang Kun explained that Bao Zheng was coming to Chenzhou on an inspection tour and he would be given the task of assassinating him. A rash, simple-minded man, Xiang Fu agreed without hesitation. "I have received your boundless favor," he declared in a loud voice. "I am willing to go through fire and water to repay your kindness, not to mention the mere assassination of someone!"

Jiang Wan hastily beckoned him quiet. "Brave man, please lower your voice! No one else must know our plan!"

"You are being too cautious," said Pang Kun. "What stranger dares to come into my garden?"

Pang Kun's lack of caution was the beginning of his downfall. At that very moment a man dressed in black was hiding outside the window and listening to every single word spoken by the people in the hall. The man was none other than Zhan Zhao, known as Swordsman of the South. A native of Wujing County in Changzhou Prefecture, he was adept in martial arts and always ready to draw his sword to uphold justice and help the weak.

Zhan Zhao roamed the country doing chivalrous deeds. When passing Chenzhou, he was struck by the misery of the people, so he made a night foray into the garden of the Marquis of Anle in search of incriminating evidence. Unexpectedly, he heard all about Pang Kun's assassination plot against Lord Bao. Zhan Zhao had met Lord Bao once and had been impressed by his honesty, impartiality, and devotion to justice.

The three men continued their discussion. In Jiang Wan's opinion, the plan must be executed without delay. Pang Kun said, "Mr. Jiang, you may take him with you and tell him what to do. Be very careful. Keep this a secret!"

The governor agreed and took his leave. Pang Kun said to Xiang Fu, "You will be handsomely rewarded after you finish the job." Xiang Fu promised to do his best and left the hall following Jiang Wan.

It was very late at night and the garden was shrouded in misty moonlight. The two of them walked only a short distance when Xiang Fu said, "Wait a minute, Your Excellency. I've dropped my hat."

Jiang Wan stopped to wait. Xiang Fu searched the ground for a while and found his hat a few steps away. He picked it up and put it on again. Jiang Wan asked, "You were wearing the hat squarely on your head. Why did it fall off to such a distance?"

"I must be walking too fast," said Xiang Fu. "My hat was caught on a twig and bounced off."

They resumed walking. Suddenly Jiang Wan said, "Brave man, there seems to be the shadow of a man over there."

"Where is it?" asked Xiang Fu.

Jiang Wan pointed with his finger. Xiang Fu gazed intently for a while, then smiled. "Your Excellency, you didn't see very clearly. It is a vertical piece of decorative rock. In the dark it looks like a man."

"I can't see very well in this darkness," admitted Jiang Wan.

"Though you can't see clearly, I can," boasted Xiang Fu. "A great master taught me the ability to see things in total darkness. Look, we have the peony nursery on the left, the lotus pond on the right, and a moon-shaped gate ahead of us leading to the outer studio."

As he said this, he touched his head with his hand. "Please wait a minute. My hat has fallen off again."

Jiang Wan stopped and turned. "Why did it fall off again?"

Xiang Fu squatted down and looked back carefully. Failing to find anything suspicious, he picked up his hat. "Well, I didn't tie my hat properly, so the wind blew it off." Even as he said this, he felt very nervous. He put on his hat and placed a hand on it to prevent it from falling again. They went out of the garden. The governor mounted his sedan chair and Xiang Fu got on a horse. Together they headed for the *yamen* of Chenzhou.

Actually, it was Zhan Zhao who had caused Xiang Fu's hat to drop twice in order to test his agility. Though he grew a bit suspicious, Xiang Fu did not respond very quickly. Zhan Zhao thus concluded the man would not pose much of a threat to Lord Bao.

Hearing cases along the way, Lord Bao and his retinue finally reached Tianchang Town not far from Chenzhou. They had just settled down in the official guesthouse when Bao Xing called outside the door, "Where does this note come from?"

Lord Bao ordered him to bring the note. It read, "Beware of an assassin at Tianchang Town. When leaving Tianchang Town, send out two bands of men, one to Donggaolin to seize Pang Kun, the other to Guanyin Nunnery to rescue the abducted women." The note was unsigned.

The note was in fact from Zhan Zhao. He had trailed Jiang Wan and Xiang Fu to the former's *yamen* that night. The following morning the governor sent Xiang Fu off to head for Tianchang Town. The governor himself hastened to meet the marquis and told him that Xiang Fu seemed to be a foolhardy man who might fail in his assassination attempt. In that case, he suggested, the marquis should disguise himself and leave for the capital by way of Donggaolin to seek refuge in his father's residence. As for Jin Yuxian and other young women in the garden, they could be taken to Guanyin Nunnery first, then transported to the capital by boat. Learning of this plan, Zhan Zhao hurried to Tianchang Town and warned Lord Bao by an anonymous note.

Having read the note, Lord Bao thought for a while, then sent for Gongsun Ce and gave him the note to read. "Search the guesthouse thoroughly and tell the guards to be alert at night," he ordered. "In addition, get two groups of men ready to set out. This message seems to be true—it must have been sent by someone sympathetic to us. We must not ignore his warning."

When they learned that an assassin was coming, Wang, Ma, Zhang, and Zhao all clenched their fists in preparation. Many guards were dispatched on sentry and patrol duty all over the place. At dark, a patrol suddenly shouted, "Look out! There's someone in the tree!"

Hearing this, the runners rushed over to the big elm

tree in the center of the courtyard. Under the light they saw a hefty man dressed in black. They tried to hit him by shooting arrows and throwing bricks, but the man dodged nimbly, moving from one branch to another. Suddenly, he caught hold of a branch and swung himself off the tree onto the roof of the house and, in a few bounces, landed on the roof of the room where Lord Bao was staying. Though Wang, Ma, Zhang, Zhao, and the other runners were all trained in martial arts, none of them could leap onto walls or roofs. They could only remain on the ground while the man began throwing roof tiles at them. Retreating to the outer wall, he was about to jump off and escape when he let out a loud cry and fell to the ground. The runners rushed over, tied him up tightly, and took him to Lord Bao.

Lord Bao was sitting in his room, casually dressed. When Xiang Fu was brought in, he hit upon an idea. Smiling, he said, "What a resolute fellow! A brave warrior like you should offer your service to the emperor instead of acting as an assassin!" He turned to Gongsun Ce. "Mr. Gongsun, please untie him for me."

Gongsun Ce realized at once what Lord Bao had in mind, but he feigned surprise, saying, "This man has been sent to murder you. How can we set him free?"

Lord Bao smiled again. "You don't understand. For a long time I've been searching for brave men whose service can be useful to the state. This is exactly the kind of man I've been looking for. He certainly bears no grudge against me, and I am sure he doesn't want to be an assassin. He was undoubtedly tricked into it by some petty men. I understand it well. Just untie him quickly!"

"Listen carefully," Gongsun Ce went up to Xiang Fu and said to him. "But for His Excellency's generosity, you would surely be put to death because of your assassination

67

attempt. Since His Excellency has shown great mercy to you on account of your talents, you must try your best to repay his kindness." He then bade the runners untie Xiang Fu.

By deliberately referring to him as an assassin, Lord Bao and Gongsun Ce effectively prevented Xiang Fu from offering any excuse for his behavior, such as pretending to be a robber. In addition, Lord Bao also used words of admiration to give Xiang Fu the illusion that he would not be punished and would even be given a position if he confessed to his crime. In this way, Lord Bao was able to get an easy confession from an otherwise hardened criminal.

Wang Chao standing beside Lord Bao also caught on to it. Finding a small arrow in Xiang Fu's leg, he said graciously, "Good friend, let me take this out for you."

Xiang Fu had no choice but to plant his feet firmly on the ground while Wang Chao took hold of the arrow and pulled it out. Xiang Fu frowned and could not help moaning painfully. Lord Bao said to Gongsun Ce, "I think this is a very brave and upright man. I would like to employ him, but I don't know if he is willing. Mr. Gongsun, please ask him about it."

"Why need we ask him?" said Gongsun Ce. "He would no doubt jump at the opportunity to serve Your Excellency. But let me ask him anyway."

On hearing all this, Xiang Fu was filled with remorse. He regretted having offered his service to the Marquis of Anle. He thought to himself that if he could become a runner in the *yamen* of Kaifeng Prefecture he would have the chance to become an official, thereby bringing honor to his ancestors. Thereupon he prostrated himself before Lord Bao. "I deserve 10 thousand deaths for offending Your Excellency! But you have not only pardoned me but given me a chance to serve you. I am more than willing to be your servant!"

Zhao Hu and some other runners were angered by Xiang Fu's words, but Wang Chao beckoned them quiet. Lord Bao was delighted that Xiang Fu had fallen into his trap. He said, "Please get up, brave man! May I have your honorable name?"

"My name is Xiang Fu, and I offered my service to Marquis Pang not long ago. The marquis was very worried when he learned of your coming visit to Chenzhou to investigate the relief mission, so he plotted with Governor Jiang and sent me to kill you. I have acted in such a shameful way, and yet you have forgiven me. I have no place to hide!"

"There's something you don't know, Mr. Xiang," said Lord Bao. "The Marquis of Anle and I are like brothers to one another. How could he want to harm me? There must be some misunderstanding caused by someone trying to stir up troubles." Then he smiled. "All this can be attributed to the unbounded favor His Majesty has bestowed upon me, which has made me so famous as to arouse the jealousy of some petty people. Mr. Xiang, I hope you will give testimony when I meet the marquis in a few days so that I can maintain my good relations with him and show my respect to his father, Preceptor Pang, whom I acknowledge as my teacher."

Xiang Fu, filled with gratitude, agreed to do whatever he was told. Lord Bao ordered, "Find a doctor to treat this brave man's arrow wound."

Gongsun Ce took Xiang Fu away, and the runners also retreated. Lord Bao told Wang Chao to stay. "You must keep an eye on Xiang Fu without being noticed," he said. "Don't let him get away!"

Wang Chao agreed. He then displayed the small arrow

he had pulled out. "Your Excellency, this arrow belongs to Zhan Zhao, the Swordsman of the South."

Lord Bao took the arrow and examined it closely. Heaving a deep sigh, he said, "The note we found also came from him. This Swordsman of the South has been helping us all along!"

The following morning Lord Bao set out for Chenzhou. In the meantime, he sent Ma Han, Zhang Long, and Zhao Hu with some men to go to Donggaolin and Guanyin Nunnery.

Lord Bao arrived in Chenzhou and settled in at the official guesthouse. Ma Han returned with Jin Yuxian and other young women seized by the marquis. A short time later Zhang Long and Zhao Hu brought back Pang Kun and his followers, after a fierce skirmish at Donggaolin.

Lord Bao immediately convened a trial. When the runners brought in Pang Kun, bound with an iron chain, Lord Bao cried out in mock surprise, "How can the bunch of you be so impertinent as to chain the marquis? Take the chain off!"

The runners hurried over to take off the chain. Accustomed to being surrounded by a contingent of guards and servants, Pang Kun was totally at a loss all by himself. He was about to kneel when Lord Bao came up and stopped him. "Please don't! Though I cannot let private interests get in the way of my official duties, I am after all your father's disciple, and you are like a brother to me."

Lord Bao returned to his seat. "However, there are some cases that I have to ask you about. You must tell the truth so that we can find a proper solution. Please don't try to conceal the facts for fear of being prosecuted."

With this, he bade Tian Zhong and the 10 old men to be brought in. He also sent runners to summon Jin Yuxian along with the other young women, and Tian Qiyuan from the prison, and sent someone to invite Jiang Wan, the governor.

After that, Lord Bao took out the written complaint of the 10 old men, called the roll, and had them vent their grievances one by one in front of Pang Kun.

Lord Bao's words showed such partiality and were spoken in such a mild tone that Pang Kun felt much reassured. He thought to himself, "Black-faced Bao must have brought me here because there are too many people suing me. He just wants to ask me some questions by way of appeasing these troublesome people, then he will surely find a way to get me out of this. I can simply go ahead and confess to everything. After that, I can ask him to let me off for the sake of my father. All officials shelter one another; even black-faced Bao can be no exception." Therefore he said, "Your Excellency, there is no need to interrogate these people. I have been misled into doing all this, and now it is too late for me to repent! Please pardon me on account of the friendship between our families! I will be forever grateful!"

Then he confessed to all the crimes he was accused of. Lord Bao had his confession recorded carefully.

After that, Lord Bao asked, "Your Highness, since you have admitted to all that, I have still another question for you. Who sent Xiang Fu?"

Staggered, Pang Kun was speechless for a few minutes. Finally he muttered, "I don't know. Governor Jiang Wan might be behind this."

Thereupon Lord Bao ordered Xiang Fu to be brought in. Xiang Fu entered the hall dressed in everyday clothes, looking not the least like a prisoner. Lord Bao said, "Xiang Fu, repeat your testimony in front of the marquis."

Xiang Fu walked up to Pang Kun. "Your Highness,

there is no need to deny it. Since Lord Bao already knows everything, the best choice is to confess."

Reluctantly, Pang Kun admitted that he had sent Xiang Fu to assassinate Lord Bao.

Lord Bao told Pang Kun to sign his confession. He complied, having no other choice.

Just then a runner came in to report, "The witnesses have arrived."

Lord Bao ordered the young women to be ushered into the hall to meet their family members. Many of them broke into tears at this family reunion. Tian Qiyuan was at last reunited with his wife, Jin Yuxian, and met his loyal servant, Tian Zhong.

After that, Lord Bao ordered, "Well then, take them down to wait for my verdict." They were taken to stand on both sides of the gate.

Lord Bao said to Pang Kun, "Your Highness, because of what you've done, you should be escorted back to the imperial capital. However, that would result in three inconveniences. First, it is a long way from Chenzhou to the capital, so you would have to take a tiring journey. Second, on your arrival in the capital, you would be submitted to the Ministry of Justice and put to interrogation with torture. Third, after the trial a report would be sent to His Majesty, who might become so angry after reading it as to impose harsh punishment on you. In that case, you would have no way of escape. Due to these three inconveniences, it would be better for you to be tried here straightaway. What do you think?"

Pang Kun thought to himself that Lord Bao must have devised a plan to save him, so he agreed hastily. "Whatever Your Excellency says, I dare not disobey."

As soon as he said this, Lord Bao cried, "Very good!" All of a sudden his face grew stern and awesome, and his voice extremely harsh. "Bring in the imperial choppers!"

At his order, the runners responded with a thunderous roar as four of them carried the dragon chopper into the hall. Wang Chao walked up and took off the yellow cover to reveal the chopper. The blade glistened under the light, the whiskers of the dragon-head shaking slightly.

At the sight of the chopper Pang Kun was scared out of his wits. He opened his mouth to speak, but Ma Han came over with four runners, pushed a wooden gag into his mouth, stripped off his garment, and placed him on a reed mat. Unable to struggle, Pang Kun was rolled up in the mat and tied with a straw rope. Zhang Long and Zhao Hu carried him over and placed him midway under the chopper. Wang Chao took the handle of the chopper and looked at Lord Bao, waiting for the signal. With a sweep of his sleeves, Lord Bao issued the order: "Execute!"

Wang Chao leaped up and brought his weight down onto the chopper, cutting Pang Kun in half. Four runners wearing white belts came up and carried off the two pieces of corpse. Zhang Long and Zhao Hu wiped the chopper clean with a piece of white cloth.

The people standing at the entrance to the hall realized beyond doubt that Lord Bao would not let anything stand in the way of justice. But the bloody scene also made them tremble with fear. Most covered up their faces and turned away, not daring to look. Some closed their eyes and began chanting the name of Buddha.

Lord Bao bade the dragon-chopper be taken away and replaced by the dog-chopper, then shouted another order, "Seize him!" At this, Wang Chao and the other runners dashed up to grab Xiang Fu. The execution of the Marquis of Anle had already filled Xiang Fu with horror. When the runners rushed toward him, he became limp with fright and could only cry weakly in protest, "What do you seize me for?"

"You treacherous ruffian!" said Lord Bao harshly. "I am a court official sent by His Majesty, and you attempted to assassinate me. How can you deny your guilt?"

Xiang Fu realized there was no escape for him. The runners carried him to the dog-chopper and executed him on the spot.

At this juncture a runner entered to report, "Your Excellency, I searched the governor's residence at your order and found he had hanged himself to escape punishment. I beg Your Excellency to send men to confirm it."

"So that scoundrel found an easy way out," remarked Lord Bao.

The case was thus concluded. Lord Bao sent away the victims after doling out compensation where necessary, and summarized the case in a petition to the emperor. He sealed the petition along with the written complaint and the signed confession and had them sent to the capital. He stayed on in Chenzhou, where he began allocating relief supplies according to the number of people in each household. Upon hearing the news, people who had fled their home gradually returned.

The emperor, on reading Lord Bao's report, made a favorable comment. From then on, however, Pang Ji began to hold a deep grudge against Lord Bao.

An Interlocking Murder Case
Uncovered by a Pig Head

Sanxing Town in Yexian County was a small but densely populated town bustling with business. Baijiabao Village to the east of the town, because of its location off the main road, was relatively quiet and peaceful. Lady Han, widowed half a year before, had just moved there with her 16-year-old son, Han Ruilong. They rented a walled courtyard with three rooms and settled down there.

Lady Han was a diligent and hardworking woman. She bade her son study the classics in the east room while she busied herself with needlework, which she was quite good at, in the west room. Mother and son seldom went out, and they hired no maid. They could barely get by on the income from Lady Han's needlework.

One evening Han Ruilong was reading by an oil lamp when he happened to look up and catch a glimpse of someone entering the west room by lifting the curtain door. The man appeared to be dressed in green and wore a pair of red boots. Han Ruilong's heart sank. He hastened to the west room, only to find his mother sitting alone by the window with her needlework. At the sight of him she asked, "Ruilong, have you finished your homework?"

"Not yet," muttered Han Ruilong. "I was thinking about a classical allusion but could not remember its origin. I need to look at the books."

He went to the book chest and began to leaf through some of the books, but actually he was looking up and down the room for a trace of the man. Failing to find

anything, he picked up a book from the chest and returned to the east room, perplexed. "I did see someone entering the west room," he thought to himself, "but no one could be found. How strange!"

That night he tossed and turned in bed, listening attentively, but no sound came from the west room. The following morning, when he went to wash his face in his mother's room, he again failed to spot anything suspicious.

At nightfall Han Ruilong lit the oil lamp and began to read. At it was getting late, he felt a little sleepy. Again he caught a glimpse of the same man in his green dress and red boots lifting the door curtain and entering the west room. Han sprang to his feet and rushed into the west room. "Mother!" he called out. Lady Han, who was doing her needlework, gave a start and stood up. "What's the matter, Ruilong? Why did you shout so loudly?"

There was definitely no trace of the man in the room. Han Ruilong stood there, confused, not knowing what to say. Lady Han realized something was wrong. "Last night you also burst in like this and thought nothing of scaring me," she said. "What's happening to you?"

Unable to find an excuse, Han Ruilong decided to tell the truth. "Mother, I saw someone entering your room just now, but when I hurried over I could find no one. The same thing happened last night."

Lady Han was astounded. "So my son has become suspicious of my behavior!" she thought to herself. "There is nothing in this room except this bed," she said. "It would be awful if someone should be hiding there. Come on, Ruilong. Bring the lamp over and take a good look."

Lady Han intended thereby to relieve her son of his suspicion. Without a word, Han Ruilong took the oil lamp in his hand and checked everywhere in the room, finding nothing. When he bent down to look under the bed, he gave a start. The ground seemed to have risen. "Mother," he said, "how come the ground under the bed is so high?"

Lady Han bent to look and saw that the ground under the bed had indeed risen. "Come, let's remove the bed."

They carried the bed away to reveal the raised earth. When they brushed away the earth with their hands, a wooden chest appeared.

Excited, Han Ruilong went out to the courtyard, returned with an iron bar, and pried the chest open. It was filled with gold and silver ingots!

Mother and son stared at one another in dismay, not knowing what to say.

Han Ruilong was the first to react. Throwing the iron bar to the ground, he cried, "Mother, this is a chest of gold and silver! It must be the God of Wealth who entered your room!" He threw out his hand to the chest.

"Don't touch it, Ruilong!" Lady Han admonished. "There is something strange about all this. The origin of the chest is not clear, so we should not touch it!"

Han Ruilong drew back his hand reluctantly. Being a young boy, he had never seen so much money before and could not bear parting with it. "Mother," he said, "since ancient times many people have had the luck of digging out gold from under the ground; we are not the only ones. We did not plunder or steal to get this chest, so what's unclear about its origin? I am sure it is a gift from heaven. The god, taking pity on our poverty, have led us to find this chest. We'd better accept the gift."

Lady Han hesitated. Life was indeed not easy for them.

"All right," she said finally. "Let's assume this is a gift from the god. Tomorrow morning you can go out and buy some sacrificial meat with which we will offer sacrifice to the gods and thank them for their gift. As for this chest, let's put it back for the time being."

Delighted, Han Ruilong put the chest back and covered it with earth, then moved the bed back into place. He washed and went back to his room to sleep.

Sleep was impossible. The image of the gold and silver ingots glittering in the chest kept floating before his eyes. He tossed in bed for a long time and finally grew sleepy. Suddenly he awoke and, looking out of the window, found the day beginning to down. He hurriedly jumped out of bed and got dressed, intending to go out and buy the sacrificial meat.

It was not until he was out of the gate when he discovered it was still before daybreak. The light he had seen was only the moon shining brightly on the ground. There was no one in the street. Where could he possibly buy meat at this hour?

He turned to walk back, then stopped for fear of waking his mother. "Since I cannot fall asleep anyway," he told himself, "I'll just take a walk out in the street."

He strolled to the market, where he saw a shop in the distance already lit up. When he went near, he recognized it as belonging to a butcher named Zheng. "What a hardworking man! His shop is open before everyone else's!"

He walked to the door and knocked on it twice, saying he wanted to buy a pig head. The light suddenly went out. He shouted a few times, but no one answered him. So he turned to leave, intending to come back later. He had taken only a few steps when he heard the door open. Turning back, he found the shop lit up again. Butcher Zheng, standing at the door, asked, "Who knocked on the door? Who wanted to buy a pig head?"

"It's me, Han Ruilong! I want to buy a pig head. I'll be back later to give you the money."

"So it's you, Mr. Han. What a time have you chosen to come out! If you want to buy a pig head, why didn't you bring a container?"

"I forgot when I left home. What shall I do now? Can you lend me one?"

"All right, I will lend you a piece of cloth to wrap up the pig head. When you come again to pay me the money, bring the cloth back with you."

Zheng went into his shop and soon returned with the pig head already carefully wrapped up. He handed it to Han Ruilong, who took it and thanked him. It was not the first time that Han had bought meat from Zheng, so he did not think it necessary to open the cloth to check on it.

The pig head was quite heavy. After carrying it for a short distance, Han Ruilong felt so sore in both arms that he had to put it on the ground and sit down to take a rest. After that, he picked it up and continued walking.

He was panting heavily when he ran into two local constables on night duty. The constables grew suspicious about such a young man gasping for breath and holding a blood-stained pack in his hands, so they accosted him. "Wait! What is it that you are carrying?"

Han Ruilong put it down. "It's a pig head."

As he was panting heavily, his words did not sound very clear, and this intensified the suspicion of the constables. While one of them lifted up the lamp, the other bent down to open the packet. Han Ruilong squatted, trying to get his breath back.

Under the moonlight and lamplight, the content of the packet was plain as plain can be. It was not a pig head. Instead, it was a loose-haired, blood-stained woman's head.

The two constables stepped back in horror. When Han Ruilong caught sight of the head, he uttered a loud cry of alarm and tumbled to the ground.

The constables, recovering from the shock, seized Han Ruilong, who was staring blankly and unable to utter a single word. The constables wrapped up the head and escorted Han to the *yamen* of the county magistrate.

By the time they arrived at the *yamen*, it was already daybreak. The constables went in and reported the case to the magistrate, who hastened into the principal hall. Drums were beaten to announce the opening of the trial. When Han Ruilong was brought in, the magistrate was surprised to see a frail-looking young boy. Instead of intimidating him with a harsh voice, the magistrate assumed a mild tone and spoke very slowly. "What's your name? Where did this woman's head come from?"

Scared into tears, Han Ruilong replied, "My name is Han Ruilong, and I live with my widowed mother. Early this morning I went to Zheng's shop to buy a pig head. As I had no container with me, Zheng wrapped up the head with a cloth and gave it to me. I took it away without opening it to have a look. Later I was stopped by these two constables. They opened the pack and discovered the woman's head in it." After saying this he burst into tears again.

The magistrate immediately sent some runners to seize Butcher Zheng. When Zheng arrived, he claimed he had not sold a pig head to Han that morning. When asked about the cloth, he said, "The cloth is really mine, but I lent it to Han Ruilong three days ago. How could I have known that he would use it to wrap a woman's head in and bring me trouble!"

Han Ruilong was too staggered to say anything. The magistrate realized there was somthing false in Zheng's words. He could not bring himself to use torture against Han Ruilong, so he had both Han and Zheng detained. The case was suspended until further evidence could be found.

Han's mother suffered a heavy blow at the news of her

son's imprisonment. She hurried to the *yamen*, asking to see her son, but the runners would not let her. She was only able to find out that her son was involved in a case about a woman's head. On her way home she came upon a procession heralded by many horsemen holding placards warning passers-by to stand aside. Recognizing the words "imperial envoy" on the placards, Lady Han threw herself onto the road and uttered loud cries of "injustice!"

Lord Bao ordered the sedan chair to stop, and Bao Xing went up to inquire what was the matter. As Lady Han had prepared no written complaint, she was brought to Lord Bao and recounted orally how her son had been detained in a murder case. Hearing her out, Lord Bao told her to return home and await his summons.

When Lord Bao arrived at the official guesthouse, the county magistrate was already waiting there. After taking a short rest, Lord Bao invited the magistrate into his room.

When asked about Han Ruilong, the magistrate said, "The case is still under investigation. No conclusion has been reached yet for lack of evidence."

Lord Bao bade him bring the witnesses to the guesthouse. The magistrate took his leave in a hurry to carry out the order.

Soon Han Ruilong and Zheng arrived. Lord Bao chose to interrogate Han Ruilong first.

Han Ruilong came in, trembling with fear, his face smeared with tears.

"Han Ruilong, why did you commit murder?"

"Your Excellency, I am wronged! I went to buy a pig head at Zheng's shop but forgot to take a container with me, so he wrapped up the head with a piece of cloth. How could I have known he had placed a woman's head inside! There is no doubt that Zheng has murdered someone and is trying to lay the blame on me!" He burst into tears again.

"Stop crying, young man. When did you encounter the constables after buying the pig head from Zheng's shop?"

"Just before daybreak."

"Just before daybreak? Why did you go out so early to buy a pig head? What did you want it for?"

At this, Han Ruilong knew he had better tell the whole truth, so he described to Lord Bao how he had seen a man in green dress and red boots enter his mother's room on two successive nights, how they had dug up a chest of gold and silver under the bed, how his mother had tried in vain to persuade him not to touch the gold and silver, and how he had got up so early to buy a pig head to offer as a sacrifice to the god.

After hearing the story, Lord Bao thought to himself, "It would be natural for a young boy like this to get all excited finding a large fortune. He does not look like a murderer to me." He bade Han Ruilong be taken away, then said to the magistrate, "Honored magistrate, you must take some people with you and go to Han Ruilong's house. Find the chest of gold he mentioned. Examine it carefully." The magistrate received the order and left the guesthouse without delay. To make haste he abandoned his sedan chair and rode off on a horse.

Zheng was brought in. Lord Bao found him a strong and fierce-looking man. When Lord Bao asked Zheng about the woman's head, he resolutely said he had not sold a pig's head to Han Ruilong. Lord Bao had to bid Zheng be taken away.

Not long after, the magistrate returned. "At the order of Your Excellency," he said to Lord Bao, "I searched Han's house and found the chest buried under the bed. When the chest was opened, the gold and silver ingots turned out to be funerary money made of paper. We also made another discovery. When the chest was removed, the headless body of a man was found underneath."

Surprised, Lord Bao asked, "By what weapon was the man killed?"

The magistrate was staggered by the question. "Your Excellency, when I saw it was a man's body without a head, I neglected to examine how he was possibly killed."

Lord Bao was highly displeased. "Why don't you find out everything you can when you go out to investigate a case? Weren't you being neglectful?"

The magistrate's face turned red at this chastisement. He admitted his mistake and took his leave. Once out of the guesthouse, he found himself covered in a cold sweat. "What a formidable imperial envoy!" he muttered to himself. "From now on I must be extremely careful, otherwise my future could be ruined."

Lord Bao had Han Ruilong brought in again. "Han Ruilong, is the house you and your mother live in a legacy from your grandparents or did you had it built yourselves?"

"Your Excellency, the house is rented."

"When did you move in?"

"No more than a month ago."

"Who lived there before you moved in?"

"I don't know."

Lord Bao bade Han and Zheng be kept in separate cells.

Could there be a connection between the female head and the headless male body? Lord Bao turned the question over in his mind but could find no solution. He became so absorbed in this case that he neglected his daily meals.

When Zhao Hu discovered the case was weighing heavily on his master's mind, he decided to help Lord Bao by cracking it himself. Without telling anyone, he disguised himself as a beggar and went to the market in search of clues.

At first Zhao Hu felt high-spirited, mixing with all the peddlers and household servants. After two days of fruitless search he began to grow anxious. As he was dressed up like a beggar, many people in the neighborhood shunned him or shut their doors on him.

By the third day, Zhao Hu had almost given up hope. As it was getting dark, he decided that this would be his last night he would spend outdoors as a beggar. The following morning he would return to the guesthouse and resume his respectable living. While he walked along the wall of a courtyard he suddenly saw someone leap into it. His spirits rose. "Excellent!" he thought to himself. "There is a thief inside. Let me go and find out what he's up to."

He threw away his stick, bowl, and ragged shoes and leaped onto the wall. Sliding down by a pile of firewood, he stopped to look around and found the man crouching behind a stack of hay. Zhao Hu dashed over and pinned the man to the ground. The man cried out in alarm, but Zhao Hu whispered harshly, "Don't shout, or I'll strangle you!"

The man felt relieved to hear Zhao Hu's voice instead of that of a ghost. "I won't, I won't," he said repeatedly. "Please spare me!"

Straddling him, Zhao Hu asked, "Who are you? What have you stolen? Where have you put it? Now talk!"

The man, taking Zhao Hu for another thief, cursed his bad luck. "My name is Ye Qian'er. I have an 80-year-old mother at home, and it's to support her that I have taken up this trade. Good friend, I have just come in and made no gains. Please let me off this time!"

"The man's words are reasonable," Zhao Hu thought to himself. "I came inside immediately after him, so he could not have stolen anything." He stood up and looked around. Under the moonlight, a piece of white silk emerging from the ground caught his attention. He took hold of it and pulled. The earth was not solid, and more and more of the silk came out until it suddenly stretched tight. Zhao Hu gave a forceful pull, and out came a pair of bound feet.

Amazed, Zhao Hu walked over, took hold of the two feet, and pulled with all his might. It was a female body without a head!

Zhao Hu turned and seized Ye Qian'er, who had just gotten to his feet. "You brazen pest, trying to mislead me to cover up your crime! Listen carefully: I am none other than Zhao Hu, working for Lord Bao of Kaifeng Prefecture. I've been lying under cover for three days to catch you, the murderer!"

Ye Qian'er was flabbergasted. In a piteous voice he whimpered, "Mr. Zhao, I am indeed a thief, but I've never killed anybody! I don't know anything about this body!"

"Who has the time to listen to your quibbling? I'll tie you up first!" Zhao Hu tied Ye Qian'er tightly with the white silk and, to prevent him from shouting, tore off a piece of cloth from his ragged trousers and stuffed it into his mouth. "Good boy, wait here patiently. I'll be back soon!"

With this he climbed up the pile of firewood, vaulted the wall, landed outside the courtyard, and started running bare-footed toward the official guesthouse.

The guesthouse was heavily guarded and well lit by lanterns hanging everywhere. When a beggar was seen running over, the four guards at the gate went up to stop him. "What a bold beggar you are! How dare you come to create trouble at this place!"

Instead of pausing to explain, Zhao Hu brushed the guards aside and dashed in. Hearing the noise, Bao Xing came out to take a look and was suddenly seized by the beggar. "Quick, tell His Excellency I want to see him!"

Bao Xing was astonished, then recognized Zhao Hu's voice. Lifting up a lantern, he was amused to see Zhao Hu dressed in ragged clothes, his face smeared with ash and dust. "Zhao Hu, where did you get this wonderful dress of yours?"

"Save your laughter. Take me to His Excellency at once. This is very urgent!"

The two of them entered Lord Bao's room. At the sight of Zhao Hu, Lord Bao was also surprised. "What happened to you?" he asked.

Zhao Hu replied that he had spent the past three days disguised as a beggar in search of clues to crack the case. He described how he had run into Ye Qian'er and discovered a headless female body.

The news delighted Lord Bao, who had been worrying over the lack of progress in this murder case. He immediately sent four runners to the house to guard the body and bring back Ye Qian'er. The four runners, informed of the house's location by Zhao Hu, set out forthwith. Lord Bao thereupon said a few words of appreciation to Zhao Hu, who smiled happily and felt very proud of himself.

A short time later, Ye Qian'er was escorted back to the guesthouse. When the piece of cloth was taken out of his mouth and the silk band unfastened, he was taken into the hall.

"What's your name?" asked Lord Bao. "Why did you commit murder? Tell the truth!"

"Your Excellency, my name is Ye Qian'er, and I have a very old mother at home. Because I am too poor to support my mother, I have no choice but to be a thief. What bad luck for me to be caught the very first time! Your Excellency, please spare me. I won't do this again!"

"You acted against the law by stealing," said Lord Bao.

"Why did you do something even worse by killing someone?"

Ye Qian'er denied the charge, saying, "Your Excellency, it is true that I am a thief, but I really didn't kill anyone!"

Lord Bao slammed the wooden block on the desk with a loud bang. "What an oily-tongued thief! Faced with the evidence of the woman's body, you still dare deny your crime. Well, take him down and give him 20 strokes of the birch!"

The runners swarmed up, pushed Ye Qian'er to the ground, and gave him 20 heavy strokes of the birch. Ye Qian'er howled and screamed, his skin badly bruised from the beating. Filled with fear and anxiety, he muttered chokingly, "Why should I, Ye Qian'er, suffer such rotten luck again and again? It's so unfair!"

On hearing this, Lord Bao demanded, "So what bad luck did you suffer last time? Speak!"

The runners roared in unison, "Speak! Speak!"

Ye Qian'er realized he had put his foot in his mouth. "Well, last time...last time I ...." He mumbled a few words but said nothing.

"He seems to need some more beating to speak fluently," remarked Lord Bao. "Take him down and give him another 20 strokes!"

Terrified, Ye Qian'er waved both his hands frantically. "No, Your Excellency! Please calm your anger! I will speak! I will speak!"

He rubbed his eyes, cleared his throat, then began his story. "Last time it happened like this. In Baijiabao there lived a wealthy man named Bai Xiong. On his birthday I went to his house to run errands for him and help him entertain the guests, hoping to get rewarded with some money, or at least some leftover food. Unfortunately, the head steward of the house, Bai An, was even more tight-fisted than his master. After the feast, he did not give me a single coin, and he would not even allow me to help myself to the leftovers. The more I thought about it the more indignant I grew, so that evening I went to the house to steal...."

Lord Bao interrupted him. "Didn't you say it was your first time when you were just caught? Or was it actually the second time?"

"Please calm your anger, Your Excellency! Stealing in Bai Xiong's house was my first time."

"What did you steal? Speak!"

"I knew the house quite well," continued Ye Qian'er. "I slipped in through the main gate and hid myself in the east room where Yinniang, Bai's concubine, lived. I knew Bai Xiong treated her as his favorite and let her keep many of his valuables. As soon as I had hidden myself, Yinniang entered. She got undressed, blew out the lamp, and went into the mosquito tent. I had to wait patiently for her to fall fast asleep. But a moment later someone knocked on the window. Yinniang slipped out of bed and opened the door. The man who entered was Bai An, the head steward. The two of them grinned like idiots and went to bed together. I said to myself, "All right Bai An, so you have betrayed you master by sleeping with his concubine! I'll steal something this evening, and tomorrow I'll come back to blackmail you." After they had fallen fast asleep, I began to move. I pried open the chest and put my hand inside. My hand touched a wooden box that felt very heavy, so I took it and left the room, thinking it must contain some valuables.

"When I returned home, I found the box was locked and a key was hanging on the side. I was more than ever convinced that I had made myself a big fortune. But when

I opened the box, what should I see but a human head!

"Last time I stole a human head, and this time I ran into a headless body. That's why I said I had suffered bad luck again and again. I must have offended the gods somehow!"

Lord Bao asked, "The head in the box, was it male or female?"

"It was a man's head."

"Where is it now? Did you bury it yourself, or did you report to the local constable?"

"I did not bury it myself, nor did I tell anyone. There was an old man named Qiu Feng, who lived in the same village as me. Once I went to steal melons from his field, he caught me. So...."

"You went to steal his melons? So when you were caught, it was your third time as a thief?"

"I am sorry, Your Excellency, stealing melons was my first time. This old man, Qiu, was very cruel. After he caught me, he gave me a severe flogging with a thick rope dipped in water. Of course I hated him, so I just went and flung the head over into his courtyard."

Lord Bao immediately sent four runners to seize Bai An and Qiu Feng. Ye Qian'er was then thrown into prison.

Early the following morning Lord Bao had just got up when one of the runners dispatched to watch over the woman's body returned in a hurry. He reported, "I went to guard the headless body last night. I waited until dawn and found it is the backyard of Butcher Zheng's house. So I have come back to report this to Your Excellency."

Lord Bao immediately sent for the the county magistrate and told him to check the body. It matched the woman's head. Lord Bao went to the main hall and had Butcher Zheng brought in.

"What a vicious butcher you are, Zheng! You killed the woman and tried to shift the blame onto someone else. You said you knew nothing about the woman's head, but her body buried in your backyard has spoken the truth. How do you plan to deny this?"

Zheng was flabbergasted to learn the body had been uncovered. He thought Lord Bao must have sent men to search his house. In the face of this incriminating evidence, he decided to confess to save himself from a heavy beating. After a long pause, he said, "All right, I'll tell everything. One day I got up at the fifth watch and prepared to slaughter a pig. Suddenly a woman knocked on the door and cried for help. I opened the door at once and let her in. Then I heard many people running outside. Someone said, 'She must have hid herself somewhere. Let's come back during the day to search the place thoroughly. We will surely find her.' After the noise of the crowd died down, I lit the lamp to take a closer look. It was a very young woman. I asked her why she had run away. She replied that her name was Huanniang. She had been abducted and sold into a brothel, but she refused to receive customers. Later, the son of a local official offered to buy her to be his concubine. She pretended to be willing and kept offering him wine until he was dead drunk, then she ran away.

"She was young, pretty, and dressed in very fine clothes made of silk and decorated with pearls. I tried to seduce her, but she cried out in alarm and resisted me, so I picked up a knife from the chopping board intending to threaten her into submission. However, at the sight of the knife she screamed and struck out blindly, and happened to knock herself against the blade of the knife. She was so fragile that her head dropped off. I removed everything valuable from her body and buried it in the backyard. I was picking the pearl-decorated hairpins from her head when someone knocked on the door and asked to buy a pig head. I hastily blew out the lamp. Then I thought to myself, 'Why don't I wrap up the head and let him throw it away for me?' I must have been tricked by the devil to do such a stupid thing. I wrapped up the head in a cloth, lit the lamp, opened the door, and called the man back. It was Han Ruilong. He happened to have no container with him, so I gave him the woman's head all wrapped up. After he left, I came to my senses and wanted to run after him and fetch back the head, but I was afraid to run into further trouble. I told myself that Han was young and timid. If he threw the head away without telling anyone, nothing would ever happen to me. If he should report it to the *yamen*, I would deny everything. I thought I could gain the upper hand over a child in court.

"Well, I didn't expect Your Excellency would be so wise as to find the body in my backyard. I have nothing more to say. All my life I have slaughtered pigs, and the first time I killed a woman by mistake I was caught. I haven't even had the chance to enjoy my spoils! What a piece of bad luck!"

Lord Bao made Zheng sign his confession and had him taken back to prison.

A runner came in to report that Qiu Feng had arrived.

Qiu was an old man in his sixties. When asked if he had buried the head in secret, he was too afraid to deny it. "That night, when I heard a thumping noise outside, I thought it might be a thief, so I went out to the backyard to take a look. There was no one in sight, but I saw a small black thing lying on the ground. I went over and picked it up. I was scared out of my wits! It was a human head! I hurried to wake up Hou San, my hired hand, and tell him to bury the head for me. But he refused to do it, saying I would be charged for murder unless I paid him 100 taels of silver. I gave him 50, and he went away and buried the head."

"Where did he bury it?"

"I don't know. You have to ask Hou San."

"Where is Hou San now?"

"He is in my house."

Lord Bao ordered the county magistrate to take Qiu Feng with him to find Hou San and dig up the head.

Bai An was then brought in. Lord Bao looked down to see a well-dressed, handsome young man. "Are you Bai Xiong's head steward, Bai An?" he asked.

"Yes, I am."

"How does your master treat you?"

"He treats me as if I were his blood kin. I could not have become what I am but for his kindness and favor."

"Really?" Lord Bao smiled coldly. "Then why do you repay his kindness with ingratitude and betrayal?"

Bai An turned pale with fright. "What do you mean by that, Your Excellency? I have always been a law-abiding man!"

Lord Bao bade Ye Qian'er be brought in.

Ye Qian'er walked in and caught sight of Bai An. "Uncle Bai," he said, "you have come at last! I have told His Excellency all about what you did. That evening you knocked on the window and entered the east room, where Yinniang lived. I happened to be hiding there. When you both fell asleep, I opened the chest and stole a hard wooden box. I had hoped to make a fortune, but the box had only a man's head in it. I don't know what business your master and you have been up to. Anyway Uncle Bai, you'd better tell the truth. I am not making all this up to blackmail you, am I?"

Bai An was stupefied by these words.

"Bai An," urged Lord Bao. "Whose head was that? Tell the truth!"

Bai An's face turned deadpan. Crawling forth on his knees, he replied, "Your Excellency, I will confess everything. The head belonged to Liu Tianlu, my master's young cousin. When my master was poor, he borrowed 500 taels of silver from Liu, but never paid him back. One day Liu came to visit and my master treated him to a feast. At the table Liu mentioned he wanted the money back, but my master tried to evade the topic and kept offering him wine. Soon Liu got drunk and began to tell us about something strange that had happened to him. On his way he had met a daft monk who gave him a so-called immortal pillow. Liu said the pillow was a fabulous treasure; if you sleep on it, you will dream of beautiful gardens with exotic flowers and jade pavilions where immortal maidens dwell. When my master heard about this, he wanted to seize the pillow. What's more, he didn't want to pay his debt. So with my help, he strangled Liu to death."

"Why did you cut his head off?"

"When Liu was dead, my master told me to bury the body somewhere in the three storerooms. At that time I was already having an affair with Yinniang, and I was worried that we would be discovered someday. So I cut off Liu's head, filled it with quicksilver, and placed it in a wooden box, which I hid in Yinniang's room. If I should get into trouble with my master, I could always use the head to blackmail him. I don't know why Ye Qian'er stole that box of all things! What back luck!"

"In which room was the body buried?" Lord Bao asked.

"After the body was buried there, the room began to be haunted, so no one dared go into it. My master separated the three storerooms from his house and closed them up into a small backyard, which he rented to the mother and son of the Han family."

Bai An was made to sign his confession and taken away. Bai Xiong was then summoned.

At this moment the county magistrate returned. "I escorted Qiu Feng to seize Hou San and dig up the head. The site was near a well. We dug at a spot Hou San marked out and unearthed a male corpse rather than a head. The corpse had a deadly wound in the forehead caused by a spade. I demanded Hou San give an explanation, and he said it was the wrong place; the head was buried somewhere else. We dug again and found the head. It had been filled with quicksilver. I dare not draw any conclusion from all that, so I have brought Hou San and the witnesses back for Your Excellency's interrogation."

After hearing him out, Lord Bao was pleased with the magistrate for showing better sense than before. "You must be tired after so much work," he said. "Please return home to rest."

He then ordered Hou San to be brought in. "The body buried by the well, where did it come from?" Lord Bao asked Hou San.

Aware that it would be futile to deny it, Hou San decided to tell the truth. "Your Excellency, I have been nervous day and night ever since I did that, so I'd better confess now. The male corpse is my young cousin, Hou Si. On that day I got 50 taels of silver from the old man, Qiu, and went to dig a pit to bury the head. But somehow Hou Si found out about this. I had just finished digging the pit when he suddenly came up and said to me, 'Hey, how do you want to be punished for burying a human head in secret?' I was scared and begged him not to tell anyone. I said I would give him 10 taels of silver. But Hou Si was not satisfied. I then offered to give him half of the silver, but again he refused. 'How much do you want?' I asked him. Hou Si was so greedy that he wanted 45 taels. I grew very indignant. I was only given 50, and he wanted 45 of it! How could I possibly put up with that? And he was so insolent! I pretended to give in but said to myself that I would bury him along with the head. I told him to dig a hole and make it big. He was very pleased after I agreed to give him 45 taels, so he began to dig with all his might. How could he have known he was digging his own grave? I waited till he had almost finished, then, when he was not looking, I struck him in the forehead with the spade. He just slumped into the pit. I buried him on the spot, then dug a small hole nearby to bury the head. When we went to dig up the head today, I was so nervous that I pointed out Hou Si's burial place by mistake. I didn't realize my error until his corpse was dug up. What I did must have been guided by the gods; there is no escape for me!"

Bai Xiong was also brought in, and what he said bore out Bai An's confession. He also handed in the so-called immortal pillow. All the criminals had been caught, and the multiple murder case was thus entirely solved.

Lord Bao gave his verdict. Butcher Zheng was sentenced to death for murdering Huanniang. Bai Xiong was sentenced to death for murdering Liu Tianlu. Hou San was sentenced to death for murdering Hou Si. All three were to be beheaded. Bai An was sentenced to death for betraying his master, committing adultery with his master's concubine, and aiding in the murder of Liu Tianlu. He would be hanged. Ye Qian'er was sent into exile for throwing the head into Qiu Feng's courtyard and bringing trouble to him. Qiu Feng was sentenced to exile for burying a human head in secret and for bribing his servant to evade punishment. Yinniang would be sold and the proceeds would go to the county treasury. The county magistrate would normally be dismissed for allowing such serious crimes to occur in the area under his jurisdiction, but he was permitted to retain his position because of his diligence and effort in resolving the case. Lady Han deserved recommendation for encouraging her son to study and for adhering to her principles even at the sight of money. For this she was rewarded with 30 taels of silver from the county treasury. Han Ruilong was chastised for harboring unfounded suspicion about his mother, but he was exempted from punishment due to his young age.

After the trial of this multiple murder case, people in Yexian County enjoyed more peace and security. Thieves no longer dared sneak into houses in the dead of night to steal wooden boxes which might contain valuables. The butchers in the market suffered a drastic decline in business. Pig heads were still available in the shops, hanging over the chopping boards and swinging in the wind, but for a long time no one came to buy them.

Exchanging a Leopard Cat
for a Prince

Near Chenzhou there was a place called Caozhouqiao
—"Bridge over Meadows," but the river had long since
dried up, and no grass grew on the banks. The place was
no more than a poor village. With a small elm tree grove
in the east, a hill in the west, and a ramshackle kiln in the
north, the village had 20-some households altogether who
barely managed to make a living. In the south lay a road
leading to the county seat, and near the road stood the
Tianqi Temple, the tallest building in Caozhouqiao. However, the residents there were too poor to offer alms, so the
monks had all gone away. Later, a Taoist priest, having no
better place to go, settled down there and became the
keeper of the temple.

The most forlorn place in the village was undoubtedly
the broken-down kiln in the north. It had fallen into
disuse for many years and had only one resident, a blind
old woman who was not native to the village. Apart from
the fact that she was distantly related to Qin Feng, a
former head eunuch in the imperial palace, the villagers
knew nothing about her. They did not even know her
name.

To tell her story, it is necessary to go back 30 years. At
that time a villager named Qin Feng served as the head
eunuch in the rear palace, so that the Qin family became
quite well-known in Caozhouqiao. One day several men
suddenly arrived at the village with a blind woman. They
were sent by Qin Feng to escort the woman to the Qin

family, with instructions that she should be accorded the same solicitation and respect his own mother received. Nothing more about the woman was revealed.

After arriving at the Qin family, the blind woman seldom spoke, nor did she ever mention anything about her past. She often fell into a gloomy mood and sometimes would burst into tears. In spite of her blindness, she conducted herself in a way that suggested good breeding and some experience of the world. Because of Qin Feng's instructions, his mother and the other members of the family treated her well. As Qin Feng served at the palace, they knew they had better not ask about her past. Soon afterwards news came that Qin Feng had burned himself to death in the palace. Hearing this, the blind woman just sat there and wept silently for a long time. Overwhelmed by grief, Qin Feng's mother died not long after. Without a head, the Qin family split up, leaving the blind woman homeless. Fortunately, she got help from an old household servant of the Qin family named Fan Sheng. Honest and sincere, he had worked in the Qin family for many years doing odd jobs and had been treated very kindly by the blind woman. Now that the family had split up, Fan Sheng offered to take the blind woman to live in his own house, but she refused. Fan Sheng then thought of the old kiln. When asked, the blind woman replied she was only too willing to go there. So Fan Sheng tidied up the kiln and helped her move in. And there she lived for the next 30 years.

After the blind woman moved into the kiln, Fan Sheng often went there with his son to help her. In times of bad weather he would prepare some food and bring it to her. The villagers came to know that a blind woman who had seen better days was now staying at the kiln and living on alms. When there was leftover food in the family, they would take it to her. Thus the blind woman was able to get by with enough to eat. Because she was blind, she had no intention of leaving the village and was content enough to settle down in the broken-down kiln.

Later, Fan Sheng died of illness and old age. Before his death he said to his son, Fan Huazong, "You must take good care of the old woman living at the kiln. She must have a very unusual background, otherwise Mr. Qin would not have her brought to his family. Furthermore, I was well-treated by her when I worked for the Qin family. After I die, you must support her well and treat her as an elder of our own family!"

Fan Huazong kept his word to his father and took good care of the blind old woman who lived on at the kiln in loneliness and peace. That dark and lonesome place had become her home.

With relief food duely distributed to the famished people in Chenzhou, Lord Bao went on an inspection tour of the nearby areas. One day he arrived in Caozhouqiao. As there was no guesthouse nearby, he had to put up in the Tianqi Temple.

Lord Bao sent for the local constable, who was none other than Fan Huazong. He appeared to be in his thirties as he stood holding a bamboo pole in his hand. Lord Bao inquired about conditions in the village, then gave Fan Huazong an official notice board to carry on his shoulder and told him to go and notify the villagers to come to the Tianqi Temple if they had any grievances to air.

With the notice board on his shoulder, Fan Huazong headed for the elm tree grove. "Brother Zhang, do you want to sue anybody?" he asked a man from the Zhang family. Then he went to the Li family. "Li the second, have you suffered any wrong?"

However, everyone reacted to his enquiry with curses. "Why should I want to sue anyone when I am living in peace? You are the constable; of course you want to benefit from other people's trouble. Get away from here, or we'll sue you!"

"Don't blame me, my fellow villagers! This is not a joke. I am just carrying out an order. If you don't trust me, look at this notice board. I am running errands for the imperial envoy. How dare I disobey?"

He made his way to the hill where people again greeted him with curses and ridicule. Not in the least discouraged, he went on to the north. An idea occurred to him. "How stupid I was!" he muttered. "There is no need to go from door to door. I can simply shout loudly."

Coming to the old kiln, he shouted at the top of his lungs, "Imperial Envoy Lord Bao has come to the village on his inspection tour and is staying at the Tianqi Temple. Whoever has suffered any injustice can go there to make his complaint!"

After shouting these words a few times, he heard someone answering him. "I have suffered an injustice! Take me there!"

Fan Huazong looked to see where the voice had come from and could hardly contain his astonishment. "Oh, old woman, you must be poking fun at me! Why should you want to complain about anything?"

Leaning against the wall, the old woman felt her way out of the kiln. Fan Huazong hastily walked up and supported her with his hand. "Old woman, what injustice have you suffered? Whom do you want to sue?"

"My son is unfilial to me. I want to sue him!" declared the woman in a clear voice.

Astounded, Fan Huazong said, "You must be confused, old woman! When did you have this son? Where could he be?"

"This son of mine.... Well, it will take a really good official to try this case. From what I have heard, this Lord Bao is an upright official especially good at dealing with complicated cases. I have been hoping for a chance to meet him. Thank heaven, the chance has come today! If I don't go and complain to him now, I will never have another chance!"

As she said this, tears welled up in her eyes and Fan Huazong tried to comfort her, saying, "All right, all right, don't cry. I will take you there." Supporting her by the arm, he headed for the Tianqi Temple. As they walked on he said to her, "Grand old woman, since you cannot see, you can hold one end of this bamboo pole when we arrive there. When I pull on it, you must fall on your knees to salute the imperial envoy. Otherwise you will get me into big trouble."

When they came to the temple, Fan had the woman wait outside while he went in to see Lord Bao. "Your Excellency, when I went to notify the people living around the elm tree grove and the hill, none of them seemed to have any injustice to complain about. Only an old woman, who is poor and blind and living in a broken kiln, said she had suffered a wrong."

"All right, bring her in."

Fan Huazong scurried out and said to the old woman, "All right, grand old woman, I have told His Excellency about you, and he asks you to go in. Please remember to kneel as soon as I pull on the bamboo pole. Don't cause me blame!"

"You don't have to worry," said the old woman. "I am not entirely ignorant about how to meet an official."

They entered the temple and walked to the west hall where Lord Bao was seated behind a desk. Fan Huazong pulled on the bamboo pole, but the old woman paid no attention to him. Fan grew anxious and pulled again and again, but the old woman responded by pulling the pole over. Fan Huazong had no choice but to kneel by himself. "Your Excellency, I have brought the blind woman."

Bao Xing, who stood beside the desk, thought the two were too close to Lord Bao. "Step back!" he shouted. "Step back!"

Hearing this, the old woman spoke before Lord Bao could say anything. "Your Excellency, please send away your servants. I have something to say."

Lord Bao sent away Fan Huazong and all the others except Bao Xing. "There is no one else here. If you have any grievances, you may speak freely now."

The old woman stood there, choked with tears. At last she blurted out, "You can't imagine what hardships I have been through, Honored Minister Bao!"

At these words, Lord Bao sprang to his feet, terribly startled. Bao Xing also shuddered in trepidation. The woman had addressed Lord Bao as if she were the empress!

Filled with apprehension, Lord Bao could only stare at the old woman, who stood there weeping silently. After a while he regained his composure. He walked up to the old woman and bade Bao Xing bring a chair for her. The old woman sat down, but Lord Bao, uncertain about her identity, remained standing beside her to listen to her story.

It all happened more than thirty years before. A misfortune befell the imperial palace, bringing about the separation of an imperial prince from his mother.

After dozens of years of peaceful rule, the Song Dynasty had achieved a measure of prosperity when Emperor Zhenzong ascended the throne. The emperor was satisfied with the service of his officials, and the common people enjoyed a good livelihood. At the morning audience on a mid-autumn day, Wenyan Bo, Director of Astronomy, reported to Emperor Zhenzong, "When I watched the sky last night, I discovered the emergence of the Heavenly Dog, which may pose a threat to the imperial princes. I have drawn a star diagram. Please take a look at this, Your Majesty."

Emperor Zhenzong looked at the picture and smiled blandly. "According to this picture, there seems to be a warning from heaven. However, I have no son now. How can the Heavenly Dog cause any harm?"

Despite this, Emperor Zhenzong's heart was heavy when he returned to the rear palace. After the empress's death, no one had been chosen to replace her. Two concubines, Lady Li and Lady Liu, were pregnant. Could the Heavenly Dog be a threat to either of them? He wanted to send for the two concubines, but it happened that both of them came without being summoned. After saluting him, they stood on either side. Emperor Zhenzong said, "Today Wenyan Bo, the Director of Astronomy, reported that the Heavenly Dog has appeared in the sky and may cause harm to the imperial princes. Though I have no offspring now, both of you are pregnant and will give birth to an imperial child. Therefore I will give each of you a dragon gown to ward off the evil influence of the Heavenly Dog. I will also give each of you a gold ball. This pair of gold balls were given to me by my late father; each contains a nine-turn pearl inside and is a priceless treasure. I have worn them since childhood to keep away evil spirits. Today I will give them to you."

The two concubines expressed their gratitude. The emperor took off the pair of gold balls, handed them to Chen Lin, the head eunuch, and bade him take them to the Director of Palace Seals and have the two ladies' names inscribed on them.

That evening the two concubines gave a banquet at the imperial garden to enjoy the moon with the emperor. After they were half drunk, Chen Lin arrived with the gold balls. Emperor Zhenzong took them in his hands and read the carved characters on them: "Lady Li of the Yuchen Palace" and "Lady Liu of the Jinhua Palace." Pleased, he handed the balls to the two concubines. After kowtowing their thanks, the two ladies put on the balls, then offered a toast to the emperor, who accepted and downed two cups. He was now totally drunk. "Whichever of you gives birth to the first imperial son will be made empress, and the son will be the crown prince," he declared with a smile.

The emperor had made this remark inadvertently. Little did he suspect that it would sow the seeds of great distress.

At that time Lady Li was superior to Lady Liu in rank. Lady Liu, a narrow-minded, jealous woman, grew anxious on hearing the emperor's remark for fear that Lady Li would be made empress by giving birth to the first imperial son. Back in the Jinhua Palace, she summoned Guo Huai, the head eunuch, and plotted with him to get rid of Lady Li.

Lady Liu had a trusted maid-servant named Kou Zhu, who was, however, an honest and upright person. On hearing of Lady Liu's secret plot with Guo Huai, she became alarmed. After that, she kept a wary eye on their activities.

Entrusted with the secret mission, Guo Huai found a midwife named You Shi, made her his sworn sister, and kept in touch with her. The midwife had never dreamed of such good luck as having a head eunuch as her sworn brother, so she tried her best to curry favor with him. After some time Guo Huai believed he had the woman under control, he told her of the plot against Lady Li, with the promise that when Lady Liu became empress, everyone who had helped her would enjoy boundless wealth and honors.

You Shi, the midwife, was delighted and readily agreed to do whatever she could. The next day she came back and told Guo Huai of a plan she had worked out. Guo Huai was so pleased that he showered praises on her. Then he went and reported to Lady Liu. They decided to carry out the plan when the time came.

In the third month of the following year, both concubines were near childbirth. One day Emperor Zhenzong was in the Yuchen Palace chatting with Lady Li when it suddenly occurred to him that his younger brother, the Eighth Prince, would be celebrating his birthday the next day. He called Chen Lin and bade him prepare a box of fruits and take it to the Eighth Prince as a birthday gift. When Chen Lin left, Lady Li suddenly knitted her brows and placed both hands on her stomach, with a painful look on her face. Aware that she was on the brink of childbirth, the emperor left and ordered Lady Liu to go to the Yuchen Palace with a midwife.

On receiving the order, Lady Liu told Guo Huai to go and find You Shi, the midwife, while she hurried over to the Yuchen Palace first. When Guo Huai found You Shi, she was well prepared. She handed him a large wicker suitcase in which she had placed a skinned leopard cat. With Guo Huai holding the case in both hands, the two of them entered the Yuchen Palace unimpeded. The guards dared not stop them to check and simply assumed the case contained nothing but food.

Lady Li was suffering labor pains when they came into the room. After a while, she gave birth to a baby boy, but she lost consciousness from the loss of too much blood. This gave Lady Liu and You Shi a good opportunity to carry out their plan. They took the skinned cat out of the case and placed the newborn baby, wrapped up in a dragon gown, into the box.

The box was then given to Kou Zhu, who had received instructions to take the case to the Jinshui Bridge in the rear garden, where she would strangle the baby with a belt and throw it into the river.

Kou Zhu walked to the bridge and opened the case. The baby was struggling, stretching and waving its limbs. Taking the baby in her arms, Kou Zhu felt her heart thumping wildly, and she was at a loss what to do. She did not want to disobey Lady Liu, yet she could not bring herself to act against her conscience and kill the emperor's son. Faced with such a dilemma, she was driven to the verge of despair. "There is no way out for me," she said to herself. "I'll just drown myself and the prince in this river to show my loyalty."

She was walking to the river when someone came up in her direction and it was too late for her to conceal herself. On a closer look, she recognized the man as Chen Lin. "Good!" she thought. "The prince will live!"

Chen Lin, ordered by the emperor to prepare some fruits, returned with a fruit box decorated with golden threads. He was surprised to see the newborn baby in Kou Zhu's arms. After Kou Zhu explained the whole story to him, he could hardly believe his ears. But the baby wrapped in the dragon gown testified to the truth of her words. Chen Lin knew he must not underestimate Lady Liu's influence in the palace. It was difficult for Lady Li to explain herself now. He had to keep the matter a secret for the time being, otherwise it would bring about great chaos in the imperial court.

Without hesitation, he opened the fruit box and put the baby into it. He told Kou Zhu to return and report she had killed the baby.

Then he covered the fruit box and sealed it. As he was walking to the palace gate, Guo Huai stopped him. "Where are you going? Her Imperial Highness Lady Liu has sent for you. She wants to ask you some questions. Go quickly!"

Reluctantly Chen Lin went to the Jinhua Palace. He kneeled in obeisance, saying, "Humble servant Chen Lin greets Your Imperial Highness. What can I do for you?"

Lady Liu sat there, sipping the cup of tea in her hands. After a long pause, she asked, "Where are you taking this box? Why does it bear the emperor's seal?"

"I was ordered by His Majesty to prepare some fruits for the Eighth Prince's birthday. That's why the box has an imperial seal on it."

Lady Liu looked at the fruit box, then turned to gaze at Chen Lin. "Have you placed something else into the box? Speak the truth! If you don't, you will get more punishment than you can bear!"

Chen Lin suppressed his alarm and decided to take a risk. "If you don't believe me, let's take off the seal and have a look." He put his hand on the box, as if he were going to peel off the seal. Lady Liu stopped him. "All right, since it is the emperor's seal, who dares to take it off? Don't you know the rules in the palace?"

"Your humble servant dare not disobey the rules!"

Lady Liu waved her hand. "You may go now. Carry out your duty properly!"

Chen Lin picked up the fruit box and made for the door, where he found Guo Huai standing there gazing at him quizzically. He bade Guo farewell and headed for the palace gate. By the time he got outside the palace he was shivering with fear and his heart was pounding wildly.

He hastened to the Nanqing Palace, the residence of the Eighth Prince, to announce the imperial edict. The Eighth Prince came out to receive the edict and had the fruit box placed on the table. As Chen Lin had come as an imperial envoy, the Eighth Prince intended to invite him to take a seat, when he suddenly noticed Chen was on the verge of tears. Surprised, the prince asked, "What's the matter?"

Chen Lin glanced around the room. Taking the cue, the Eighth Prince sent away all his servants. Assured that no one else was in the room, Chen Lin kneeled and broke into tears. He recounted how Lady Liu had plotted against Lady Li and how Kou Zhu had saved the crown prince, who was then lying in the fruit box.

Dumbfounded, the Eighth Prince walked over to open the fruit box and take out the baby wrapped in the dragon gown. Suddenly, the baby boy started crying as if to complain of his misfortune. Hastily the Eighth Prince went into the inner room with the baby to tell his wife, Princess-Consort Lady Di. Chen Lin was also invited in and made to tell the story again. They decided to let the baby stay in the Nanqing Palace, to be brought up by Lady Di, and keep the whole matter a secret until the situation changed for the better.

Seeing that everything was well arranged, Chen Li took leave and returned to the imperial palace.

News of Lady Li having given birth to a monster spread quickly in the palace and caused much confusion. Some palace attendants swooned at the sight of the skinned leopard cat. Lady Liu lost no time in reporting the matter to Emperor Zhenzong, who became convinced that Wenyan Bo's prediction had been thus fulfilled. In a rage, he had Lady Li expelled from the Yuchen Palace and banished to a limbo called the Cold Palace, and promoted Lady Liu to Honored Consort of the Yuchen Palace.

Informed that she had given birth to a monster, Lady Li was heartbroken and overwhelmed with shame. She was too absorbed in her misery to make any protest about her banishment.

The head eunuch at the Cold Palace was Qin Feng, a kindhearted man who was not on friendly terms with Guo Huai. He did not quite believe Lady Li had borne a monster, thinking there must be another explanation for the incident. As Lady Li was filled with shame and sorrow, blaming herself for what had happened, he took pity on her and tried his best to comfort her. He also arranged for a trusted young eunuch named Yu Zhong to wait upon her and tend after her every need without fail. By a coincidence, Yu Zhong bore a striking resemblance to Lady Li. He was loyal and very dependable, so Qin Feng took him as his foster son. The two of them tried all they could to set Lady Li's mind at ease, but she kept weeping all day, too ashamed to meet anyone.

Lady Liu rejoiced at her success and highly rewarded Guo Huai and You Shi in secret. After a dozen days she gave birth to a baby boy. Overjoyed, Emperor Zhenzong immediately made Lady Liu empress and her son the crown prince. Lady Liu began to treat Guo Huai with special favor; You Shi and Kou Zhu also were promoted.

The crown prince was a lively boy, and Lady Liu loved him dearly. At the age of five, he suddenly fell ill and, unresponsive to all treatment, died a few days later. Lady Liu cried her heart out. Emperor Zhenzong was also filled with grief, lamenting that he was probably destined to have no son.

Sensing the emperor's grief, the Eighth Prince often went into the palace to visit him. One day Emperor

Zhenzong asked the prince how many children he had. In answering this question, the Eighth Prince mentioned that his third son was also five years old. His interest aroused, the emperor asked the prince to bring his third son into the palace sometime.

This was exactly what the Eighth Prince had in mind. He told Ning, the head eunuch of the Nanqing Palace, to go and fetch the third son. The third prince came and saluted the emperor properly, conducting himself with great ease. Much pleased, the emperor told the boy to come near. The boy had a familiar look he could not quite place. When asked questions, the boy replied fluently in a crystal clear voice. Cuddling himself to the emperor, he felt a natural affinity and did not appear the least afraid.

The emperor was delighted. Looking at the Eighth Prince, he said, "Eighth brother, your son is such a loveable boy!"

Seizing the opportunity, the Eighth Prince said, "If Your Majesty likes him so much, why not adopt him? How fortunate he would be then!"

Emperor Zhenzong was overjoyed. He immediately issued an edict adopting the third prince as his own son and making him the crown prince of the East Palace. The Eighth Prince expressed his gratitude and recommended Chen Lin to be the head eunuch of the East Palace to take care of the crown prince. The emperor consented.

Chen Lin took the crown prince to meet the empress, Lady Liu, and the various imperial consorts. They first came to the Zhaoyang Palace, where Lady Liu lived. The crown prince kneeled to salute Lady Liu, who pulled him to his feet. She was surprised to find in the crown prince a resemblance to the emperor. When Chen Lin said they had to go and call on the consorts, Lady Liu remarked, "All right, you may go. But afterwards, bring the crown prince here. I have to ask him some questions."

Walking past the Cold Palace, Chen Lin deliberately pointed it out to the crown prince. "This is the Cold Palace, where Lady Li lives."

"Why does she live here?"

Chen Lin explained that she had been banished here for giving birth to a monster, but she was nevertheless a very kind and virtuous woman.

The crown prince said he wanted to go in and see her. Qin Feng came out of the palace and greeted them. Chen Lin, who was a good friend of Qin Feng, introduced the newly elected crown prince. Qin Feng saluted the prince and ushered him into the palace.

Lady Li looked thin and withered, her face ravaged with grief. At the sight of Chen Lin, she burst into tears. Chen Lin also had a lump in his throat. He introduced the crown prince, who walked up to Lady Li and touched her with his hands, for even as a child he felt pity for the pathetic-looking woman living in such a squalid place and wanted earnestly to comfort her. Lady Li took the crown prince in her arms and wept bitterly.

The two eunuchs could not help feeling pity for the woman. Chen Lin, much grieved, tucked at Qin Feng's hem and led him out of the gate. "Mr. Qin, how has she been lately?"

"The same as before. She has not had a single day of joy in the past few years."

Chen Lin paused, then looked up at Qin Feng. "Mr. Qin, we have a long-standing friendship between us, and I trust you more than I trust anyone else. Lady Li's sufferings are heartbreaking. Now I will tell you a great secret. She did not give birth to a monster. The new crown prince is none other than the baby she gave birth to five years ago."

Qin Feng was astounded. Chen Lin went on to describe briefly the plot of substituting the prince for a leopard cat. Finally he said, "This is a matter of the utmost secrecy; even His Majesty has been kept in the dark. Lady Liu has ruled as empress for a long time now. If the secret should be divulged, the crown prince would certainly come to harm, and it's hard to tell what the emperor would do in his rage. Undoubtedly the entire imperial court would be plunged into commotion. Mr. Qin, you are a sensible man. Now that I've told you the truth, you can take care of Lady Li properly. When it's convenient, you can tell her about it and advise her to take care and wait for better times to come."

Both surprised and delighted, Qin Feng hurried in with Chen Lin. The crown prince was comforting Lady Li. "Auntie Li, I will ask my mother to persuade the emperor to move you to another place."

Chen Lin went over and took the crown prince by the hand. "The empress is waiting to ask some questions of you. Let's go."

They went to the Zhaoyang Palace to meet Lady Liu. At the sight of the tear stain on the crown prince's face, she asked what was the matter. The crown prince, being a small child, made no secret of what he felt. "Just now I visited Auntie Li at the Cold Palace. She looked so thin and pitiful. Please, mother, say something to the emperor so she won't suffer so much."

Empress Liu was startled but did not show it. "What a benevolent and virtuous imperial heir! All right, you can count on me. I will speak to His Majesty at the first opportunity."

She went on to chat with him for a while and could not contain her suspicion because of his resemblance to Lady Li. After the crown prince left, she immediately sent for Kou Zhu. As she remembered, Kou Zhu had been dispatched to take the baby away, and soon after that Chen Lin had left with a fruit box for the Nanqing Palace. Could the baby have been hidden in the box?

Kou Zhu arrived and saluted the empress. Empress Liu went straight to the point, asking what she had done with the baby five years before. Startled, Kou Zhu insisted that she had carried out the order to the letter. Empress Liu found Kou Zhu's reply unconvincing, so she had her tied up, suspended on a rope, and tortured to force her into confession. Kou Zhu, fully aware of the consequences of a confession, said nothing until she lost consciousness from the torture.

Her suspicion unabated, Empress Liu had another idea and sent for Chen Lin.

Chen Lin understood the situation at once when he saw Kou Zhu under torture, but he acted as if he knew nothing. Empress Liu said, "Chen, I've treated Kou Zhu well, but the faithless girl betrayed me five years ago by hiding away the crown prince. I want her to confess her guilt. Come, help me teach her a lesson!"

A eunuch came over and handed a whip to Chen Lin. Under Empress Liu's gaze, Chen Lin realized he was also under suspicion. "I'm sorry, Kou Zhu," he muttered to himself silently, and raised the whip.

Kou Zhu knew her number was up. She closed her eyes, trying to blank out her mind. At this moment a palace attendant arrived with an imperial edict to summon Chen Lin. Though unwilling, Empress Liu had to let him go.

Continuously tortured, Kou Zhu began to feel she could not longer bear the pain. Instead of being tortured to death, she preferred to die a quick death. So as soon as she was untied, she dashed to a pillar and crashed herself to death on it.

At the news, Empress Liu was dazed for a moment and a sense of remorse welled up in her heart. Since childhood Kou Zhu had waited on her with loyalty and devotion, yet she was forced into such a miserable end. Empress Liu felt pity for Kou Zhu and had her body buried in secret.

But her suspicion was far from quelled. The crown prince's visit to the Cold Palace had aroused in her both anxiety and trepidation. She began to regard Lady Li as a serious threat. She would have no peace of mind unless Lady Li was eliminated.

However, she knew it would be inexpedient to murder Lady Li outright. For the time being all she could do was send some trusted servants to pay frequent visits to the Cold Palace, both to keep Lady Li under supervision and to look for a chance to remove her.

In the meantime Lady Li continued to lament her fate and blame herself for everything that had happened to her. Qin Feng could not bear it anymore, so he decided to tell her the truth. Lady Li could hardly believe her own ears, feeling as if she had just been awakened from a nightmare. After that, she began to get better day by day. However, she knew she had to bide her time, for the life of the crown prince and stability of the imperial court was at stake.

Lady Li felt much better about herself than before. The emperor's attitude toward her no longer seemed important. Instead, she began to place her hope on her son, the crown prince. Every evening she burned incense and kneeled to pray for her son.

Empress Liu was soon informed of Lady Li's behavior. Lady Li's apparent rise in spirits filled the empress with alarm. She was more than ever convinced that the woman in the Cold Palace posed the most serious threat to her position.

Then she hit upon an idea. She would use Lady Li's evening prayers as an excuse to get rid of her.

One day Emperor Zhenzong summoned Guo Huai to inquire after matters in the rear palace. Guo Huai seized the opportunity to talk about the Cold Palace. "There is something I dare not keep from Your Majesty," he said. "Recently Her Highness Lady Li has been found burning incense every evening. She mutters some words that sound like ... like curses. I am afraid she may have become so discontented as to try and harm Your Majesty."

The emperor flew into a rage, throwing away the bowl of ginseng soup in his hand. He immediately ordered a piece of white silk to be given to Lady Li along with instructions to hang herself.

It was a bolt out of the blue. Qin Feng was staggered by the news, not knowing how Lady Li could have offened the emperor again. However, he quickly calmed down and sent someone to find his foster son, Yu Zhong. Then he went to see Lady Li. Hearing the terrible news, Lady Li swooned. Soon Yu Zhong arrived. Sending away the other attendants, he said to Qin Feng, "There is no time to lose. Help me change into Her Highness's clothes. Don't think of anything else. Quick!"

When he heard this, Qin Feng's eyes brimmed with tears, and he could not utter a single word. This had been in his mind when he hastily sent for Yu Zhong, but at the last moment he hesitated, unwilling to part with his foster son.

Yu Zhong began with haste to change clothes. "Father, help me, quick! Don't think too much. Father!" His eyes also filled up with tears. "Father, you have treated me so well it would never be possible for me to repay your kindness. I do not want to leave you, but think of Her Highness. I am a worthless man whose life has no more meaning than that of grass or a tree. Lady Li is different. Oh Father, Quick!"

Qin Feng knew it was the only way out. He helped Yu Zhong into Lady Li's dress and adornments, then carried Lady Li into Yu Zhong's room, putting her in bed and pulling a quilt over her. From a distance it would appear that Yu Zhong were lying ill in bed.

Soon after, a ranking palace woman named Meng arrived with the imperial edict. His eyes red from weeping, Qin Feng came out to receive her and asked her to sit down. "Let's wait till Her Highness has gone to heaven. Then we can go in and take a look."

Lady Meng was touched by Qin Feng's sadness. She used to get along quite well with Lady Li and could not help feeling sorry for her.

After a while a palace maid came out to report, "Her Highness has gone to heaven. Please come in."

Qin Feng burst out crying. Lady Meng, also in tears, walked to the door and looked inside. It appeared indeed to be Lady Li. She could not bring herself to walk up to take a closer look. "Watch over her carefully," she said. "Don't move her until I have reported the matter to His Majesty."

After that, Qin Feng wept for a whole day. He could find no one to share his sorrow over the loss of his foster son.

Lady Li finally came to and asked what had happened. Qin Feng had no choice but to tell her. He also advised her to act cautiously and not expose herself to further danger.

Listening to the story, Lady Li sat there without saying anything, as tears welled up in her eyes and rolled down her cheeks.

She was awash in tears day after day, grieving over Yu

Zhong's death, longing for her son, the crown prince, and lamenting her misfortune. It did not take long for her to become blind, engulfed henceforth by total darkness.

As Lady Li's conditions kept deteriorating, Qin Feng thought it unsafe to keep her in the palace and decided to send her to his home. He went to Guo Huai, the head eunuch of the rear palace, and said to him, "My adopted son, Yu Zhong, has fallen seriously ill. There seems to be little hope for his recovery. If he should die here, it would tarnish the palace grounds. Please let me send him to my hometown."

Guo Huai, who had never liked Qin Feng and Yu Zhong, was only too pleased to learn of Yu Zhong's serious illness. He would regard Yu's death as good riddance and did not want him to recover in the palace. So he readily gave his consent. Yu Zhong was expelled from the palace and restored to the status of commoner.

It was in this way that Lady Li had left the palace and arrived at Caozhouqiao, where she was to spend the next 30 years.

After Lady Li had left, Qin Feng remained in the Cold Palace. The death of his foster son was a heavy blow to him, and he became very ill. One night, fire suddenly broke out all around the Cold Palace. Eunuchs and palace women ran for their lives in all directions, leaving Qin Feng alone in his bed. He knew it must be another plot devised by Guo Huai. By setting fire to the Cold Palace Guo would be able to murder his opponent without a trace. Even if Qin escaped from the fire, he would be held responsible and sentenced to death. Qin Feng heaved a deep sigh and did not move in his bed.

After that, no one knew the imperial concubine of the Cold Palace was still alive, except for Lady Li herself.

Chen Lin, the Eighth Prince, and his Princess-Consort

Lady Di all knew the truth about the crown prince. But they considered it difficult and meaningless to try to reveal and prove the secret now that Lady Li was dead. So Lady Di brought up the crown prince as her own son.

Upon the demise of Emperor Zhenzong many years later, the crown prince ascended the throne. He was called Emperor Renzong.

In the Tianqi Temple the blind old woman had finished her tale. Both Lord Bao and Bao Xing were stupefied.

The old woman fumbled in her ragged clothes and brought out an oil-stained packet. Bao Xing went up and threw out his hand to take it, then stopped himself. "How can a person of my status take something directly from her hands?" Then an idea came to him. He moved close to her and lifted the hem of his dress. "Please let go!"

The old woman loosened her grip, and the packet dropped into Bao Xing's dress. He quickly handed it over to Lord Bao, who opened it layer after layer. The innermost layer was of silk with a yellow cloud design, available only in the imperial palace. Lord Bao opened it to see a gold ball inscribed with the words "Imperial Consort Lady Li of the Yuchen Palace."

Awestruck, Lord Bao wrapped up the gold ball and bade Bao Xing hand it back to the old woman on his knees, then guide the old woman to the seat of honor with the bamboo pole. With Bao Xing guarding the door to prevent anyone from bursting in, Lord Bao straightened his dress and kneeled before the old woman in obeisance. "Bao Zheng pays homage to the empress dowager! I didn't know you were here; please forgive me for not receiving you earlier!"

Lady Li held out her hand. "Honored Minister Bao, please get up. I will depend on you to redress the injustice

120

I have suffered!"

"I will do everything in my power!" pledged Lord Bao. "However, something untoward might happen unless we keep this a secret for the moment. If we are not careful, the news will get out and cause all kinds of troubles. I would suggest that I acknowledge you as my mother to prevent others from learning the truth. Please pardon my impertinence!"

"That is a good idea," said Lady Li. "You may proceed with the matter in whatever way you think appropriate."

Lord Bao stood up, beckoned Bao Xing over and whispered a few words into his ear.

Bao Xing hurried out of the temple, only to find Fan Zonghua being castigated by the county magistrate. "The imperial envoy has arrived here on an inspection tour. Why didn't you report to me at once?"

"His Excellency first asked me a lot of questions, then he sent me on a lot of errands. I just didn't have the time...."

"Stupid! How dare you find excuses for your mistake? I will break those useless legs of yours!"

Bao Xing walked up and interposed. "Come on, magistrate, let him off. It was you who came late; why should you blame him? He has been kept quite busy for a while now. He isn't the only person available in your county, is he?"

Judging by the way Bao Xing spoke, the magistrate realized instantly this must be a close follower of the imperial envoy, someone he could not afford to offend. Forcing a smile, he said, "I was not informed of His Excellency's arrival, so I am late. Please, brother, speak in favor of me before His Excellency." He turned to take his official namecard from a runner and offered it to Bao Xing with both hands. "Please, brother, pass on my regards to

His Excellency."

Bao Xing took the namecard nonchalantly. "His Excellency intended to take a look around the area and had no use for your service, but unexpectedly he has just had the joy of finding his mother. He has instructed you to prepare a sedan chair, two clever maids, and a dress of the best quality complete with hairpins and rings. Bring them here as soon as possible, for we need them urgently. As for the expense, put it in the records, and we will reimburse you once we are back in the capital." The magistrate agreed hastily.

Bao Xing turned to Fan Huazong and said with a smile, "Hey, boy, you've done something really good! The old woman you took here turns out to be His Excellency's mother. She said you have treated her very well and wanted to take you along to the capital. So you will leave with us to wait on her along the way."

Fan Huazong was delighted. He scratched his ears, lifted his eyebrows and wrinkled his nose, not knowing what to say. Bao Xing said to the magistrate, "Honored magistrate, relieve this young man of his duty. His Excellency wants his company to the capital to take care of the old lady. You'd better try to make him look more presentable—at your own expenses."

"No problem!" said the magistrate eagerly. "No problem at all!"

"Go and get things done," said Bao Xing. "Take him with you. When you have prepared all the things we need, let him bring them to us. The sedan chair can wait, but the dress, jewelry, and maids must be sent here as soon as possible."

The magistrate bowed with clasped hands. "Trust me, brother, everything is readily available. I'll go back and get it ready at once."

Sure enough, Fan Huazong returned in a moment resplendently dressed, along with the sedan chair, two maids, and a nice dress with jewelry. The dress and jewelry belonged to the magistrate's wife, and the two maids were her favorites. The magistrate, eager to please the imperial envoy, had made a lot of promises to persuade her to part with them.

Thereupon Lord Bao wrote a letter to his wife, sealed it, and gave it to Bao Xing, who set out at once for the capital. He also ordered the runners to pack up. They were to set off in a few days and head straight for the capital, making no detours along the way.

Bao Xing, riding a horse, hastened back to Lord Bao's residence in Kaifeng. Lord Bao's wife, Li Shi, who missed her husband, was startled by Bao Xing's sudden return, thinking something unfortunate might have happened. Bao Xing reported that Lord Bao was all right, then handed her the sealed letter. Li Shi opened it and read the following:

"By a great coincidence I met Lady Li, the empress dowager, mother of the ruling emperor. It is impossible to tell the whole story in a few words. I have acknowledged the empress dowager as my mother, and we will be back in the capital in a few days. She will stay in our house for a while. Please have the east room of the Buddha's shrine cleaned for the empress dowager. Upon her arrival, you must salute her in the same manner you salute your mother-in-law. This is a matter of the utmost importance to the state; on no account should you tell this to anyone else. Please remember it! After reading this letter, burn it."

Li Shi finished reading, burned the letter over a candle, and bade the servants clean up the east room of the Buddhist shrine. The room was redecorated. Two bright and sprightly maids were chosen to wait on the empress dowager. The other servants received warning that entry into the Buddhist shrine was henceforth strictly forbidden. Servants delivering food must go no further than the corridor.

Everyone at the residence learned Lord Bao had found his mother. Ready and alert, they waited anxiously for her arrival.

Two days later, a runner arrived with a message: "The old lady has entered the city and will be here soon."

Everything was well prepared. At the head of the family, Li Shi waited in the hall. The main gates were opened wide and the servants, all dressed up, stood waiting on both sides. A moment later a big sedan chair arrived, upon which all the servants kneeled in salute. The sedan chair was carried into the hall. Li Shi went up to it and had a maid open the door. The empress dowager walked out, and Li Shi fell on her knees. "An unfilial daughter pays respect to her mother-in-law!"

The empress dowager held out her hands, and Li Shi quickly took them. The empress dowager pulled at Li Shi, saying, "My daughter-in-law, please get up!"

Li Shi got on her feet and walked the empress dowager to the east room of the Buddhist shrine.

After tea was served, Li Shi said to the two maids, "You may go and rest with the servants who have come with the old lady. I won't be needing you here."

The maids retreated. With no one else in the room, Li Shi kneeled again. "Your humble subject, Li Shi, pays respect to the empress dowager. May you live a thousand years!"

The empress dowager hastily took Li Shi by the hands and pulled her onto her feet. "Don't act like this anymore, my dear daughter. Just treat me as your mother-in-law. There is no need, under the circumstances, to stick to courtly rules. Minister Bao has told me your family name is also Li. Why don't you be my foster daughter?"

Li Shi kneeled and kowtowed in gratitude.

On his return to the capital, Lord Bao went first to the palace to see the emperor and report about his work in Chenzhou and his inspection of various places along the way. Much pleased, Emperor Renzong said a few words of appreciation and rewarded Lord Bao with many treasures from the palace. Lord Bao expressed his gratitude and hastened home.

Back in his house, he went first to pay respect to the empress dowager, then went to see his wife and told her the story of the empress dowager.

As Li Shi listened to the sad tale, tears welled up in her eyes. She asked if the empress dowager was completely blind and if she had seen a doctor. Lord Bao said, "She went blind because of incessant weeping. Since she spent the past 30 years in a poor village, where could she have found a doctor?"

Li Shi considered. "In the village where my parents live, there is a doctor named Tao, who is very friendly with my father. From what I have heard, Doctor Tao is able to cure all types of blindness unless one is born blind or has been injured. I think maybe...."

"That's great!" exclaimed Lord Bao with delight. "There is no time to lose. Send someone to fetch that doctor at once! What a joy if the empress dowager can be cured of her blindness!"

Li Shi expressed her doubts. "The empress dowager is no ordinary patient. If Doctor Tao treats her successfully, that will be fine; if not, wouldn't we be held responsible?"

"There is no need to worry! The empress dowager has gone through numerous hardships and is a woman of virtue and understanding. I'll explain the matter to her clearly.

You just arrange for someone to fetch Doctor Tao as soon as possible."

The following day Lord Bao reported the matter to the empress dowager, who consented with pleasure. "You and your wife have taken so much trouble for me! If my eyes can be cured and I can see the sky and the sun again, it will be a gift from heaven and a proof of your loyalty and devotion!"

Soon afterward, Doctor Tao arrived. Learning the patient was Lord Bao's mother, he took extra care in his treatment. For more than 20 days the empress dowager took oral medicine and had ointment applied to her eyes. One day Doctor Tao, after applying the usual dose of ointment, went to bid Lord Bao and Li Shi good-bye. "When the bandage is taken off tomorrow, the old lady will be able to see. You may trust me in that. I will take my leave now." Lord Bao and Li Shi were about to speak when Doctor Tao beckoned them silent. "This has been my long-time habit. I want to make blind people see the light, but I don't want them to see me. I like my name to be spread far and wide but my face to remain unknown. Well, forgive this little idiosyncrasy of mine. I will take my leave now. Please pass on my regards to the old lady!"

He bowed with clasped hands. Lord Bao and Li Shi walked him out of the hall and dispatched a runner to escort him back to the village.

The following day Li Shi sent away the maids and went personally to unwrap the bandage for the empress dowager. Then she brought a bowl of water. After washing off the ointment, the empress dowager opened her eyes tentatively and felt stabbed by a strong light. She closed her eyes quickly, then opened them again slightly. After a few times she became used to the light. Her eyes wide open, she looked around and saw Li Shi standing before her. Overjoyed, the empress dowager took Li Shi by both hands. "My daughter! I see you at last!"

Hearing this, Lord Bao, who had been waiting outside the door, knocked lightly. Li Shi hastened to open the door and let him in. Lord Bao went up to the empress dowager and kneeled in salute. "Your subject Bao Zheng offers his congratulations! May you live a thousand years!"

The empress dowager, elated, told Lord Bao to raise his head. What she saw was a black, square face with long ears, a big mouth, and a pair of large, protruding eyes. He looked the very epitome of good fortune and majesty.

The empress dowager, gazing at Lord Bao, thought of her own son. Her eyes brimming with tears, she said in a choking voice, "I have benefited so much from your help! I will depend on you both for what remains to be done!"

Lord Bao comforted her, saying, "There is no need to worry. Your humble subject will do his best and proceed with great caution. The injustice will be redressed, and the dignity of the imperial court restored!"

Almost a month had passed since Lord Bao's return to the capital, but still he had taken no action concerning the empress dowager. Fortunately, Lady Li understood the situation quite well and remained patient. Lord Bao went to pay respect to her every day, and Li Shi went there more often to wait upon her and keep her company.

One day Bao Xing came in to report that Ning, the head eunuch of the Nanqing Palace, requested to see Lord Bao. The Eighth Prince had been dead a long time, but his wife, Lady Di, was still alive. The Nanqing Palace was presided over by his son, Prince of Liuhe.

As Lord Bao had made it a rule never to cultivate relations with members of the imperial clan, he waved his hand to Bao Xing and bade him send Ning away. However,

Li Shi stopped Bao Xing and whispered a few words to Lord Bao, who nodded his head, saying, "You are right." He turned to Bao Xing: "Take Mr. Ning to the studio."

Li Shi had talked to Lord Bao about the empress dowager. As Lady Di was one of the few people who knew about the incident of the leopard cat, Ning's call gave them a very good opportunity. It would be most desirable if a meeting between the empress dowager and Lady Di could be arranged. After all, people all over the empire recognized Lady Di as mother of the ruling emperor.

Bao Xing went out and said to Ning, "My master invites you to come in to the studio!"

Hearing this, Ning burst into a broad smile. Following Bao Xing into the house, he said, "That's what I expected, you know. Your master would certainly honor me with his presence, due to our long relationship!"

Bao Xing curled his lips and thought to himself, "What relationship is he talking about? I have served my master for many years, but I have never seen any relationship between my master and him!"

They entered the studio and tea was served. A short moment later Lord Bao came in. After an exchange of greetings, Lord Bao asked, "What do you have to teach me, supervisor Ning, having come to my humble place?"

Ning produced a smile. "I am not here on any official duty. My master, the prince, admires you deeply for your uprightness and capability, and Lady Di often instructs him to follow your example to become a virtuous, upstanding prince. He has long wanted to meet you and benefit from your company, but has not yet had the chance. Now Lady Di's birthday is coming soon. Why don't you prepare a small gift and bring it to our house? In this way you will be able to reciprocate Her Highness's regards for you and satisfy the needs of our prince. What do you think of this?"

"When is Her Highness' birthday?"

"Celebrations will be held tomorrow, though the birthday actually falls on the day after tomorrow. That's why I have hurried here to make this call."

"Thank you for your kind instruction," said Lord Bao, "and I will certainly follow it. However, there is one thing I need to ask you about."

"What is it?"

"As an official of the outer court, I am not fit to meet Her Highness face to face on her birthday. It happens that my mother is now staying in my house. I think it might be better for me to send the gift tomorrow, and the day after tomorrow for my mother to visit in person. Would that be appropriate?"

"Oh, so your mother has come to the capital? That would be even better! I will go back and report to Her Highness."

"Thank you for taking the trouble," said Lord Bao. "When my mother comes to visit, please take good care of her."

"Trust me!" said Ning with a smile. "I will certainly do my best. We have enjoyed a long-standing relationship, haven't we?"

Lord Bao saw Ning to the gate. He came back, described his conversation with Ning to his wife, and asked her to inform the empress dowager. Bao Xing was ordered to prepare a simple birthday gift of peaches, noodles, candles, and wine.

In the meantime Li Shi went to the east room of the Buddhist shrine to see the empress dowager. After hearing her out, the empress dowager looked a bit uneasy. "My daughter, I have nothing to worry about except this: What sort of dress shall I wear, and how shall I greet Lady Di? I shall be so ashamed if this is not done properly!"

Li Shi kneeled to reply. "You have to deign to wear a garment of the second official rank. When you arrive there, I don't think Lady Di will sit motionless to receive your salute. You can act according to the circumstances and try to get around that. Lady Di will certainly not take offense because of that. When you see the chance, tell her the truth. Everything will be fine then."

The empress dowager thought for a long time. Finally she said, "Oh well, given the present situation, there seems to be no other choice for me."

The next day Bao Xing rode on horseback to the Nanqing Palace accompanied by a runner carrying the birthday gift. The street before the palace gate was crowded with carriages and sedan chairs. There were people everywhere carrying gifts in their arms or over their shoulders, creating quite a racket. Bao Xing had to dismount and ease his way to the gate. One by one the visitors handed their namecards and gift lists to the guards at the gate, speaking in soft voices and bowing and nodding incessantly. The guards, however, looked haughty and indifferent. At the sight of this Bao Xing's heart sank, for the gift he had brought appeared just too shabby compared with those of the other visitors.

Reluctantly, he walked up the steps to a guard and handed him a visiting card in a respectful manner. "Please, good sir, report to your master about my visit."

The guard rolled his eyes upward to show the whites. "Well? Where are you from?"

"I am dispatched by Lord Bao of Kaifeng Prefecture—"

The guard jumped at the words "Kaifeng Prefecture" and grabbed Bao Xing by both hands. Bao Xing started.

"Is the gift from Lord Bao? Oh my good brother, thank you for taking so much trouble! Chief Ning told us this morning that Lord Bao would be sending his gift, and we have been waiting for it! Please come in and take a seat inside."

He turned to bark at a few house servants, "Why are you standing there like idiots? Go and find the gift from Kaifeng Prefecture and carry it inside. Hurry up!"

He led Bao Xing into a room, offered him a seat, then served tea. "This morning the Prince himself also ordered us to report to him as soon as the gift from Kaifeng Prefecture arrives. Since you are here, do you want to meet the Prince?"

Bao Xing regained his calm and replied, "Well, since I am here, I'd better see him. I will have to trouble you again, honored sir."

"Oh good brother," the guard said, "please don't sir me anymore! We are good brothers, aren't we? My name is Wang San, and I am the third son of the family. Perhaps I am a few years older than you, so you can call me Elder Third Brother Wang from now on!"

With this he took the visiting card and went in to report.

Afterward Bao Xing was called in to meet the young prince, who thanked him for Lord Bao's gift and gave him a reward of 50 taels of silver.

As Bao Xing went out, the head eunuch, Ning, came up to him with smiles. "Here you are! Thank you for taking so much trouble yesterday!"

"My master sends his greetings to you," said Bao Xing. "I'm sorry for being a poor host yesterday."

"Not at all! When you return and see your master, pass on my greetings. I have reported the matter to Lady Di, who will be expecting your master's mother tomorrow. Lady Di also said she wants not so much to celebrate her birthday as to have a good chat."

Bao Xing promised to pass on the message and took his

leave. At the gate he thanked Wang San, then headed back. On his way he thought to himself, "The eight-item birthday gift I took there cost us no more than 30 taels of silver, but the prince gave me 50 as a tip. It seems that the prince does admire my master a lot."

He reported to Lord Bao what had happened, then submitted the prince's note along with the 50 taels of silver. Lord Bao read the note and handed the silver back to Bao Xing. "You have run a good errand. Since the prince gave it to you as a reward, you may keep it."

Early the next morning Li Shi got up and helped the empress dowager wash and get dressed. The sedan chair was ready. The empress dowager was about to take leave, but suddenly she was overcome with sorrow and broke into tears. Li Shi went up and comforted her. "Please don't worry anymore. The result of this visit will affect the fate of the imperial court. You will have to decide on the spot what to do and must not lose your presence of mind."

"My daughter, it is thanks to you and your husband that my sufferings will finally come to an end! If everything goes smoothly this time, I will meet you again in the palace!" She mounted the sedan chair and set off.

Bao Xing escorted the sedan chair to the Nanqing Palace. Informed of their arrival, Lady Di ordered, "I won't see any more imperial clanswomen today. Decline all visitors, say I am tired, and invite the old lady from Kaifeng Prefecture to come in."

The sedan chair was carried inside the ceremonial gate. Ning, the head eunuch, came up and lifted the curtain. "Greetings, grand mistress!"

The maids helped the empress dowager out of the sedan chair. She took a look at Ning. "Greetings, supervisor!"

Lady Di was waiting at the door of her bedchamber. She was startled by the sight of the empress dowager, who had a familiar appearance she couldn't quite place.

The empress dowager came up and acted as if she were about to kneel in salute. Lady Di hastily took her by the hands, saying, "Let's skip the formality!" The empress dowager, taking the chance, did not insist. The two of them walked into the room hand in hand and took seats.

The empress dowager gazed at Lady Di and sighed inwardly at her aged countenance. Lady Di, looking closely at the empress dowager, suddenly became aware of her striking resemblance to the imperial concubine Lady Li, who had died many years before. The discovery made her a bit uneasy.

While they chatted, Lady Di found to her delight that this "grand mistress" did not appear like an old woman from the country but conducted herself with calm and ease befitting a member of an aristocratic family. No wonder she had brought up Bao Zheng to become such an outstanding official! Much pleased, Lady Di asked the empress dowager to stay on for a few days, to which Lady Li readily consented.

Lady Di ordered a feast to be prepared. She asked Lady Li to sit by her side so they could chat more conveniently. To her delight, Lady Li acceded with no difficulty at all.

At the table Lady Di naturally said a few words of praise about Lord Bao's loyalty and talents. "All this is due to your proper instruction. You are truly admirable in this respect!"

Lady Li grew uneasy and said a few words by way of modesty, not wanting to pursue the topic. Lady Di, however, went on to ask, "How old are you, grand mistress?"

"I am 52."

"Oh, I see. And how old is your son?"

Lady Li balked at the question, her face turning red with embarrassment.

Lady Di, surprised and a bit displeased, did not press on.

After dinner Lady Li was shown around. The more Lady Di looked at her the more doubtful she became. She wondered, "Why does the grand mistress resemble the late Lady Li not only in appearance but in the way she holds herself, moves and talks? When asked about her son's age, she turned red and could not give an answer. How could a mother be ignorant of her son's age? Isn't it unthinkable? Perhaps Bao Zheng is not her natural son."

Lady Di was determined to unravel the mystery. That evening she said to the maids, "Clean up the room and get everything ready for the grand mistress, then leave. I want to speak to her for a while."

The two of them sat and chatted. Suddenly Lady Di asked, "During the day I asked about your son's age, but to my surprise you didn't know. He is not your natural son, perhaps?"

At this Lady Li fell silent. Lady Di grew impatient and goaded her, "Grand mistress, if you don't answer my question, you will be deceiving me. To deceive me is the same as to deceive the emperor. Don't you know the consequences of such a crime?"

Forced into a corner, Lady Li blurted out, "My imperial sister, can't you really recognize me?" As soon as she said this, she broke into tears and began to weep uncontrollably.

Lady Di felt as if her doubts had been verified. She asked hastily, "Are you the imperial concubine Lady Li of the Yuchen Palace?"

Lady Li was much too grieved to speak. Lady Di urged, "There is no one else in this room. Why don't you tell me everything?"

It took a long time for Lady Li to check her tears. From inside her dress she took out a gold ball and handed it to Lady Di. Lady Di examined it carefully under the lamp-light, handed it back, and fell on her knees. "Your subject didn't know the arrival of the empress dowager. Please pardon my disrespect!"

Lady Li helped her up. "Please don't, my elder sister! I have endured hardships for over 30 years without revealing my identity for fear of causing trouble. Now that I have the good fortune to meet you at last, I need your help to get in touch with my son."

Lady Di described in detail what she knew about the incident 30 years before. For the first time Lady Li learned how Empress Liu had tortured Kou Zhu to death and used slander to obtain Emperor Zhenzong's edict ordering her to commit suicide. Lady Li then recounted how she had escaped from the palace with Yu Zong's help and settled down in Chenzhou, and how she had encountered Lord Bao a month before and followed him back to the capital. As they talked, both were overcome with emotion and choked with tears.

Eager to be reunited with her son, Lady Li asked, "Imperial sister, how can my son be informed of all this, so we can enjoy a reunion?"

Lady Di thought for a moment. "The emperor, taking me for his mother, comes to the Nanqing Palace to greet me every day. If I am not feeling well, he will arrive immediately to see me. Tomorrow I will pretend illness and send Supervisor Ning to report to the emperor, who will surely come in great haste. Then I will take the opportunity to tell him the truth. What do you think?"

Lady Li nodded her approval. After that the two of them continued to chat late into the night, reliving the joys and sorrows of many years before.

Early the next morning Ning was sent for. He was ordered to go and inform the emperor that Lady Di was struck with a sudden, quite serious illness. Ning headed off without delay.

At the news Emperor Renzong became very worried. He immediately called off the morning audience and headed for the Nanqing Palace. Prince Liuhe met him at the gate. When asked about Lady Di's conditions, the prince replied, "She has become a little better." A bit relieved, Emperor Renzong told his retinue to wait outside the gate and entered with only Chen Lin accompanying him.

They came to the bedchamber, which was very quiet. Emperor Renzong was surprised. "If my mother is ill, why doesn't she have the maids around to take care of her?"

Lady Di was lying in bed inside an overhanging tent. She was dressed in informal clothes, with her face to the wall. Emperor Renzong went up and offered his greetings. At this Lady Di turned and said abruptly, "Your Majesty, of all things under heaven, what is the most important principle?"

Puzzled, Emperor Renzong replied, "It must be the principle of filial piety."

Lady Di nodded her head. "If that is the case, how can a son be ignorant of his mother's life or death? How can an emperor allow his mother to live a wanderer's life?"

Emperor Renzong was now totally confused. Staring at Lady Di, he did not know what to say and began to suspect that she was delirious. At this Lady Di said, "Your subject knows all the details about this matter and is afraid that Your Majesty might not believe her!"

Emperor Renzong was startled to hear Lady Di talk in that way. "Why do you talk like this, mother? I don't understand!"

Without speaking, Lady Di produced a box covered in yellow brocade, opened it and took out a packet wrapped tightly in yellow silk. She handed the packet to the emperor. "Your Majesty, do you know where this came from?"

Emperor Renzong opened the packet to see a gown of dragon design with the inscription "Keep the Heavenly Dog at Bay" in the late emperor's handwriting. Beside the inscription was the stamp of the imperial seal. Emperor Renzong stood up and examined the gown for a long time. Still puzzled, he turned to look at Prince Liuhe, who lowered his head and said nothing. Chen Lin, however, had broken into tears. Emperor Renzong asked anxiously, "Please, mother, where did this packet come from? Please tell me about it!"

Lady Di sat up, paused for a moment, then began to recount the tale of 30 years before. At the end she said, "Thus your mother took refuge in Chenzhou and spent the next 30 years in a broken-down kiln. Fortunately, Minister Bao, on his inspection tour in Chenzhou, met your mother at Caozhouqiao. To keep the thing a secret he acknowledged her as his mother and brought her back to the capital. Yesterday, when I celebrated my birthday, your mother took the chance to visit me."

It took Emperor Renzong a long time to recover from the shock. "In that case," he asked, "where is my mother now?"

At this moment he heard someone sobbing behind the screen. An old lady in the dress of the second official rank emerged from behind it. While Emperor Renzong just stared at her in a daze, Chen Lin let out a shrill cry and dropped to his knees.

Lady Li, seeing the emperor's confusion, handed the

gold ball to him. Emperor Renzong took the ball and read the inscription, "Imperial Consort Lady Li of the Yuchen Palace," in the same style as the gold ball worn by Empress Liu, the ruling empress dowager. Emperor Renzong was bedazzled. A short moment later he came to his senses. Moving forward, he fell on his knees. "Your son is unfilial! You have suffered so much, mother!"

Mother and son threw themselves into each other's arms and burst into tears.

Those who stood by could not help weeping. Lady Di and Prince Liuhe kneeled to comfort the emperor and asked to be forgiven for keeping the secret from him for so long. Emperor Renzong and Lady Li finally stopped crying. The emperor turned and helped Lady Di to her feet. "Please get up, auntie! I would not have been alive but for your love and care. Please let's treat each other just like before and not let formality stand in our way."

Then he pulled Chen Lin to his feet and thanked him. "Virtuous man, where would I have been today if you had not been loyal to the empire and risked your life to save me!"

Chen Lin could not speak for weeping, but kowtowed repeatedly in a mixture of joy and sorrow.

Emperor Renzong was torn by conflicting emotions of joy and grief at the reunion with his mother. "Though I am the emperor," he said, "I have allowed my mother to go through great suffering. How can I face the court officials? Won't I become the laughingstock of my people?" He stopped, choked with shame and remorse.

At this Lady Di said, "Your Majesty, please calm your anger. On your return to the palace, you can issue a secret edict and send Guo Huai and Chen Lin to read it at the Kaifeng Prefecture. Minister Bao will surely know how to wring the truth out of Guo. In this way that old rascal won't be alerted. Otherwise, though he has no way to escape, he might kill himself to evade punishment. That would be letting him off too lightly."

Emperor Renzong agreed. Back in the palace, he immediately wrote an edict himself, sealed it, and ordered Guo Huai and Chen Lin to go and read the edict at the Kaifeng Prefecture. Taking it to be a conferment of honor on Lord Bao, Guo Huai did not feel any suspicion and went with Chen Lin to Lord Bao's office.

When a runner came in to announce the arrival of an imperial edict, Lord Bao hurried to the principle hall, where Guo Huai was already standing with the edict in his hands, with Chen Lin behind him. As he was superior to Chen Lin in rank, Guo Huai thought it natural for him to read the edict. As he opened the seal, Lord Bao kneeled to listen to the edict. Throwing out his chest and taking a deep breath, Guo Huai began to read aloud, "The Emperor, who pays tribute to Heaven and rules with the mandate of the gods, enjoins the following: Guo—" He stopped abruptly at the sight of his own name. Chen Lin took over the edict and went on:

"Guo Huai is a man who cherishes vicious motives and is full of wiles. When the late emperor worried for lack of an heir, he did not show his loyalty and devotion. When Empress Dowager Li became pregnant, he set up a vicious trap. As a result, the mother of the present emperor suffered injustice for over 30 years and endured numerous hardships in a strange land. Because of his heinous crime, he is to be tried at Kaifeng Prefecture until he makes a full confession. This is an order from the emperor himself!"

Lord Bao cried "Ten thousand years to the emperor," stood up to receive the imperial edict, and placed it high on the table. He then turned and shouted an order: "Seize him!"

Zhao Hu, hearing the order, dashed toward Chen Lin to grab him, but was stopped in time by Wang Chao and Ma Han, who went up to remove Guo Huai's official hat and robe and place him on his knees before Lord Bao. Aware of his mistake, Zhao Hu turned red with embarrassment and stepped back.

After listening to the imperial edict, Guo Huai turned pale with fear. Lord Bao conducted a trial in the main hall and had Chen Lin sit by his side. A deafening shout from the runners announced the opening of the court. Lord Bao demanded, "Guo Huai, the secret plot of 30 years ago is finally uncovered, and His Majesty is enraged. How did you plot against Empress Dowager Li and exchange the crown prince? Tell the truth!"

Guo Huai began to recover from the shock. He had not served in the imperial palace for dozens of years without obtaining the presence of mind to deal with emergencies like this. At Lord Bao's question, he replied with ease, "How can you ask such a question, Your Excellency? Because Lady Li gave birth to a monster, the late emperor became angry and banished her to the Cold Palace. Where was a crown prince to be exchanged? I am truly wronged!"

Previously, Guo Huai was startled to see his own name in the imperial edict. When Chen Lin began to read it, Guo thought to himself, "So the secret has been uncovered. Though I had a hand in it, it was, after all, Empress Dowager Liu's idea. She will surely shield me. With the empress dowager to back me up, what do I have to fear! I must clench my teeth and deny everything. After a couple of trials, the empress dowager's edict will arrive and put an end to this. Without my confession, black-faced Bao or even the emperor himself will be helpless to press further.

Moreover, that concubine Li was ordered to commit suicide many years ago, so no one alive can bear witness against us. It would be unthinkable for them to dare do anything to the empress dowager!"

Guo Huai had been too absorbed in his own thoughts to listen clearly, and therefore missed the message that Lady Li was still very much alive, ready to claim the position of empress dowager for herself.

When Guo Huai denied the charge, Lord Bao said, "According to you, the monster was not a substitute. But why did you tell Kou Zhu to take the crown prince out, strangle him to death, and throw him under the Jinshui Bridge? Speak!"

"Nothing like that ever happened! I don't know anything of the sort. If Kou Zhu said that, you should ask her. But unfortunately she is dead."

Lord Bao slammed his wooden block on the table angrily. Before he could speak, Chen Lin interposed. "Chief Guo, you are not supposed to speak like that. What has been done cannot be denied. If there had been no such thing, why did Kou Zhu hand me the crown prince? I took the crown prince with my own hands—what do you have to say about that?"

Guo Huai retorted, "Chief Chen, how come you are also here to interrogate me? If Kou Zhu had handed you the crown prince, you would be the one to be interrogated. What does it have to do with me? What's more, both you and I serve in the palace. Are you not acquainted with the disposition of the empress dowager? When her edict comes in a short time, I'm afraid you'll have to pay dearly for your mistake!"

Guo Huai intended this to be a warning not only to Chen Lin but also to Lord Bao. However, Lord Bao merely responded with a cold smile, his face harsh and severe.

"Guo Huai, do you want to intimidate me in the name of Empress Dowager Liu? If you had not mentioned her name, I would perhaps take pity on you and let you off lightly. Now that you have mentioned it, you'll have to suffer the consequences!" He threw down a bamboo chip with the order, "Take him down and give him 20 heavy strokes of the birch!"

The runners roared in response and pushed Guo Huai onto the ground, beating him severely with a birch plank until he became a mass of bruises. Guo Huai clenched his teeth and did not utter a single sound. When the beating was over, it took him awhile to scramble to his feet. Lord Bao asked, "Guo Huai, are you ready to confess now?"

Aware of the odds against him, Guo Huai was determined to stick it out to the end. "Concubine Li brought punishment to herself by giving birth to a monster; no exchange ever took place. If Kou Zhu claimed the crown prince was exchanged for a monster, who can bear her out? Why should her words be taken to be true?"

"Very well," said Lord Bao. "According to you, what Kou Zhu said must not be believed. But why did Lady Liu and you have Kou Zhu flogged and tortured?"

"Because she offended Empress Dowager Liu by answering back. She was therefore punished to warn her against future offences."

Chen Lin interposed again. "Chief Guo, you have made another mistake here. When Kou Zhu was interrogated, I was ordered by Empress Liu to carry out the flogging. Empress Liu kept asking the whereabouts of the crown prince. How can you attribute all this to a verbal offense on Kou Zhu's part?"

Guo Huai gave Chen Lin a withering look. "Chen Lin! As you said, Kou Zhu was flogged because of the crown prince, but I didn't hear the empress dowager ask a question like that. You just mentioned that it was you who flogged her; well, she killed herself because she could not bear the beatings anymore. Therefore it was you who forced her to commit suicide. What right do you have to interrogate me now?"

Lord Bao put on a grim expression. "What an incorrigible rascal! What a glib tongue you have! Runners, put him in the finger clasp!"

With a loud shout the runners seized Guo Huai and placed his hands into the finger clasp. As the rope was tightened, Guo Huai was stabbed by a great pain and began to wail in agony.

Lord Bao demanded, "Guo Huai, are you ready to confess?"

His teeth tightly clenched, Guo Huai muttered, "I have no confession to make!" He was trembling all over, his face livid, beads of perspiration rolling down his face from his forehead. At the sight of this, Lord Bao feared that Guo might die if the torture continued like this. The finger clasp was removed, and Guo Huai was taken away and thrown into prison.

Lord Bao left the main hall and invited Chen Lin to the studio. He asked Chen Lin to describe what he knew about the incident 30 years before, then told him to report to the emperor about that day's trial. Lord Bao promised he would find a way to force Guo Huai to confess.

In his cell, Guo Huai was aching both in his fingers and from the wounds inflicted by the heavy flogging. He scarcely touched the food delivered by the prison guards. At the end of three days he grew very anxious. "I have stayed here for three days. Why hasn't the empress dowager issued an edict? Could she still be kept in the dark? Even if everything has been done in great secrecy, I wait on her every day. When I failed to appear for three days, wouldn't she ask about me? Wouldn't someone tell her the truth?"

After a while, an idea suddenly occurred to him. "Yes, that's it! The empress dowager must be ill these days, so she cannot think of anything else. All I have to do is staunchly deny everything. Without my confession, black-faced Bao cannot give a verdict. After another two or three days, the empress dowager's edict will surely arrive. Well, if I am destined to suffer a seven-day calamity, it will be impossible to reduce it to six and a half days. Nevertheless, I just cannot understand how the emperor learned of the matter after so many years. He issued an edict, and I ended up here! I really cannot understand how this could have happened!"

He was thinking in this fashion when he heard the prison guard shouting to him. "His Excellency has called a trial. Chief Guo, you are invited to come!" Guo Huai started, his heart thumping heavily at the prospect of another ordeal. Making an effort to collect his wits about him, he followed the runners to the principal hall.

Lord Bao looked at Guo Huai and found him thin and haggard, unlike just a few days before. He assumed a mild tone. "Guo Huai, you are now advanced in years and have no difficulty understanding the situation. Why do you persist in denying your crime? In my opinion, as Empress Dowager Liu is involved in the case, you will not take the sole blame even if you make a full confession. Why don't you tell the truth then? After that, I will submit a separate report for you and close the case as early as possible. Won't that be better?"

"What is this?" Guo Huai thought to himself. "Black-faced Bao is trying to trick me!" He assumed an earnest expression and replied, "Your Excellency, how can I talk about something that never really happened? If there had been such a plot, its very enormity would have exposed it many years ago. Please consider this, Your Excellency!"

"His Majesty has already been informed, and I know the story from beginning to end. What's the point of you trying so hard to deny it?"

"Since you know everything about it, why don't you tell me? I will admit to whatever crime you choose to accuse me of. Why is there any need to ask me about anything?"

Lord Bao went into a fury on hearing this and banged the table with his wooden block. "What a hardheaded criminal! How dare you talk back to me! Runners, bring the searing iron!"

Four runners came up and stripped Guo Huai of his upper garment. Though his face became rather thin and pallid, his body was still very fat. A runner came behind him, a red hot searing iron in hand. Lord Bao asked, "Guo Huai, will you confess or not?"

"I am waiting for your dictation, Your Excellency. Whatever you tell me to confess, I will do at once!"

Incensed, Lord Bao ordered the punishment to be executed.

With a sizzling sound the iron burned Guo Huai again and again, and a stink of seared flesh floated across the hall. Guo Huai broke into a fit of howling and wailing, but after 'a while he lost consciousness. At this Lord Bao ordered the punishment be stopped and Guo Huai taken back to his cell. He sent for the prison warden and whispered a few words of instruction to him.

After a long time Guo Huai gradually came to. He felt a burning pain all over his body, and he could hardly move his limbs. Suddenly, someone called gently beside him, "Big lord, what a rough time you've been through!"

Guo Huai, lying on his stomach, opened his eyes slightly and saw the prison warden smiling broadly, with a covered bowl in his hand. "What do you want?" he asked in a weak voice.

The prison warden put down the bowl and helped Guo Huai to sit up, then handed him the bowl. "Big lord, your servant has nothing to offer except this pill and a bowl of millet wine. Taken with the wine, this pill will relieve the pain and ease the mind."

A pain killer was exactly what Guo Huai needed most at that moment. He took the pill eagerly. In the past few days no one had paid any attention to him, so the prison warden appeared to him like a long lost friend. "Thanks so much for this. If I get out of here someday, I won't forget you."

"Big lord, you don't have to say that. When all this is over, you only need to snap your fingers to have me get all the benefits I need."

Flattery had never felt so good before to Guo Huai. He took the pill and drank the wine. After a while, he really began to feel better. "Is there any more of this wine?"

"Yes! Just a moment!" The prison warden quickly went off to refill the bowl and offered it to Guo Huai respectfully. Treated with such deference and solicitation, Guo Huai felt much better. As he drank the wine, he asked, "Have you heard of anything unusual in the palace in the past few days?"

"Nothing really unusual. The empress dowager fell ill because she was haunted by Kou Zhu's ghost, but she is already getting better. The emperor goes to the Renshou Palace to visit the empress dowager every day. It will only take a day or two for the empress dowager's edict to arrive, then you will be out of this trouble. Though His Excellency is acting on the emperor's order, he won't dare to disobey the empress dowager. As the saying goes, the arm is no match for the leg. If the empress dowager gets angry, the emperor won't dare to confront her, not to mention my master."

At these words Guo Huai felt a surge of relief and downed several bowls of wine. He had scarcely eaten anything in the past few days, so that a few bowls of wine made him tipsy and misty-eyed. The prison warden took away the bowl. "Big lord, please rest for a while. I'll come back later to wait on you."

Waving his hand, Guo Huai said in a mumbling voice, "You—may—go. Let's talk sometime later."

Though he could not speak clearly, his thoughts still lingered on what he had just heard. "This warden is a kind-hearted man. So the empress dowager is ill because of Kou Zhu's ghost. Well, Kou Zhu did die a miserable death. It's not strange at all for her ghost to haunt the palace!"

He was drifting into a daze when a strong wind arose outside and the bells hanging from the eaves began ringing. The wind grew stronger, throwing sand against the windows with a swishing noise. Guo Huai forced his eyes open but could not see clearly. The sound of the wind made him shiver with cold, so he pulled the clothes tightly around him and tried to sleep. After a while, a sobbing voice floated toward him. He half opened his eyes to peer into the darkness and caught sight of a shadow floating toward him under the moonlight. A cold shiver ran down his spine. Before he could let out a cry, he found the shadow standing right in front of him. It was a woman with dishevelled hair. "Chief Guo," she said in a whining voice, "How have you been since we last met? Don't you remember Kou Zhu?"

Guo Huai's head swam as from a heavy blow, and he was half sober from the shock. "Kou ... Kou Zhu, what ... what do you want?" he asked in a trembling voice.

"You don't need to be afraid. I only want you to bear

witness for me. Yesterday, in the Palace of Hell, the empress dowager claimed that you were the mastermind behind what had happened 30 years before, so the King of Hell agreed to let her return to the human world. Furthermore, the King discovered in the book that both the empress dowager and you still had 12 years to live in the human world. Twelve more years to go! I have waited long enough in Hell as a wandering ghost. Therefore I have come to take you to Hell to explain everything, so the case can be cleared and I can enter the next cycle of rebirth. If you don't follow me, I will come back every day to haunt you!"

As she began to move closer, Guo Huai jumped aside in fear. Though the light was dim and her face smeared in blood, he could still recognize the appearance of Kou Zhu. "As the prison warden said, she was haunting the palace," thought Guo Huai to himself. "How did she trace me here? What a smart ghost she is!" He muttered hastily, "Kou Zhu, don't trouble me with this! Yes, you were wronged and died a cruel death. I plotted with that old woman, You Shi, to exchange the crown prince with a leopard cat to create a case against Lady Li, and unfortunately you got implicated and suffered a lot. Now, since I still have 12 years to live, why don't you let me off? Once out of prison, I will invite lots of eminent monks to conduct a grand ceremony to release your soul from misery!"

As he said this, he tried to edge away from the ghost, forgetting the pain from his wounds. The ghost said, "Chief Guo, thank you for cherishing such a kind thought. When we arrive in the Palace of Hell in a moment, you only have to explain the case clearly for me to get released and reborn; no Buddhist monks or Taoist priests will be needed. If you don't tell the truth, many more troubles will arise."

At this moment two small ghosts emerged from the darkness uttering a fit of shrieks. Each had snarled red hair and a horrible-looking face, dressed in fur waistcoats, and holding notice-boards in their hands. They came to Guo Huai in leaps and bounces, shrieking loudly, "The King is out for an audience! The spirit of Guo Huai is summoned to testify for the ghost of a wronged woman!"

They grabbed Guo Huai and dragged him away. Wind was throwing sand against his face and sending shivers all over his body. His head reeling, Guo Huai stumbled along with the two ghosts over a long, winding road to arrive at a hall. It was dark and cold. Suddenly the two ghosts bellowed, "Kneel!"

Guo Huai, in a state of utter stupefaction, hastily fell to his knees. He heard a voice coming from above. "Is this Guo Huai?"

The two ghosts replied, "Yes, it's Guo Huai; there's no doubt about it!"

"Guo Huai, what you and Empress Dowager Liu did together has been recorded in the books of the Palace of Hell. Normally your lives would be terminated and both of you should be sent into another cycle of rebirth. However, you have to be escorted back to the human world since each of you has 12 years left. But there is the problem of Kou Zhu's ghost, who has been wandering for 30 years, a state not very desirable in the Palace of Hell. Therefore your spirit is summoned today. You must tell in your own words what you did. After that, the case can be cleared, and she will be reborn. As for you, you will be sent back to the human world to enjoy your last years in peace."

The voice paused, then called out, "Judge!"

"Here!"

"Bring the files and check if he's telling the truth."

The sound of paper shuffling was heard. The judge

said, "I have found the place. We can begin now."

"Good! Guo Huai, it's your turn to speak!"

Guo Huai was too befuddled to think of anything except the 12 more years he could still enjoy—if the King of Hell was satisfied with his confession. So he kneeled there and told the story in great detail, describing how he and Empress Liu plotted together against Lady Li, how they exchanged the crown prince for a skinned leopard cat, how they tortured Kou Zhu until she committed suicide, and how they slandered Lady Li to the emperor.

The King asked, "Judge, do his words match the record?"

"Yes. No great disparity is found."

"All right. Let him sign the confession and take him back!"

Two ghosts came up and handed the written confession to Guo Huai, who signed it without much hesitation, eager as he was to return to the human world.

An order was issued. "Back to the human world!"

The hall was suddenly lit up. Dazzled, Guo Huai batted his eyes and thought, "The way to the Palace of Hell is quite long; how can the way back be so short?"

He opened his eyes, only to see to his great bewilderment Lord Bao sitting high above. Beside Lord Bao stood Gongsun Ce, and on both sides were the runners from Kaifeng Prefecture. Everyone was gazing at Guo Huai, smiling.

Guo Huai seemed to become aware of something, but he did not know what it was. He simply felt as if he were falling into a bottomless pit. Blood surged to his head, and he passed out without saying anything.

Lord Bao bade Guo Huai be carried back to prison, then said to Gongsun Ce with a smile, "Well, our plan is carried out to consummation. What a joy!"

He told the "female ghost" to come up and rewarded her with 20 taels of silver. "This is to pay for your work. Take it and try to make your living in a decent way!"

Everything had been prearranged by Lord Bao a few days before. The searing iron had been applied to Guo Huai to make him suffer severe pain. Then the prison warden had been sent to tell the story of Kou Zhu's ghost haunting the empress dowager and to make Guo Huai drunk, so that he could be led to the "Palace of Hell" in a state of total stupefaction. Intimidated by the "wronged ghost" of Kou Zhu and lured by the prospect of 12 more years to live, Guo Huai had finally been tricked into a full confession.

Kou Zhu's ghost had been played by a courtesan sought out from a local brothel. She had been chosen because she looked like Kou Zhu and was quite articulate. Gongsun Ce had made her rehearse her role carefully before acting it out.

In this way, Lord Bao succeeded in obtaining a full confession from Guo Huai. At the morning audience the following day, he submitted a report to the emperor along with Guo Huai's signed confession. Emperor Renzong read the confession without making any comment. As soon as the audience was over, he headed straight for the Renshou Palace to see Empress Dowager Liu.

Lady Liu had been ill in bed for many days. In her delirium she felt herself haunted by ghosts, and she kept uttering cries of alarm. The palace women waiting upon her all became very afraid. When Emperor Renzong arrived, Lady Liu happened to be in a sober state. With the emperor standing before her, she made an effort to speak. "Guo Huai is an old official who served for many years under the late emperor. If he has committed any error, I hope you will make special allowances for him!" She had been informed that Guo Huai was on trial in Kaifeng Prefecture, but she did not know why. On hearing this, Emperor Renzong silently produced Guo Huai's confession, threw it down before Lady Liu, and turned his back to her. Lady Liu was startled, for the emperor had never treated her in this way before. She hastily opened the confession. After reading only a few lines, she was horrified. Old, decrepit, and weak from illness as she was, the blow was too hard for her to take. Choked with phlegm, she opened her eyes wide and gasped desperately for breath, then kicked her feet and breathed her last.

At the screams of the attendants, Emperor Renzong turned back. For a long time he gazed silently at Lady Liu, whose wan face showed the shock and confusion she had suffered at the last moment of her life. Then he turned away and ordered a funeral to be prepared. By his instruction, Lady Liu would be buried as an imperial concubine.

Emperor Renzong returned to summon Lord Bao and inform him of Lady Liu's death. He bade Lord Bao draft an edict notifying the entire populace of the empire of the true identities of Lady Liu and Lady Li. Only then did the common people learn that the emperor's mother was named Li instead of Liu.

Emperor Renzong had an auspicious date picked out and fasted for three days in advance, offering sacrifice to the heaven, the earth, and his ancestors. On the chosen day he went to the Nanqing Palace at the head of all his court officials to receive Empress Dowager Li back to the imperial palace.

As for Guo Huai, he woke up to find himself back in prison again. He was not interrogated again. Apart from the prison guard who brought him his three meals a day, no one took any more notice of him. He realized he had fallen into Lord Bao's trap by confessing to everything, so that no more interrogation was needed. What he did not know about was Lady Li's rehabilitation. As he recalled the bloody palace incident of 30 years before that finally resulted in his downfall, all those years spent in wealth and power seemed like a transient dream to him. He heaved a deep sigh and lowered his head.

In the meantime Emperor Renzong was radiant with joy after welcoming his mother back to the palace. Lord Bao was promoted to prime minister, and his wife, Li Shi, was invited to the palace by Empress Dowager Li to enjoy a happy reunion of mother and daughter. Emperor Renzong issued an edict giving Chenzhou a five-year tax exemption. He also bestowed a thousand taels of silver to have the old kiln in Caozhouqiao transformed into a temple, to be supervised by Fan Huazong. A tract of land was assigned to provide sustenance for the temple. The emperor also had two petition temples built in the rear palace. The one on the left, the Temple of the Loyal Martyr, was dedicated to Kou Zhu. The one on the right, the Temple of Two Righteous Men, was dedicated to Qin Feng and Yu Zhong. At the completion of the two temples, Emperor Renzong went in person to burn incense there. He promoted many officials and proclaimed a national amnesty.

The only person excluded from the amnesty was Guo Huai. The midwife, You Shi, had been dead for a long time. Lady Liu had died of shock. Only the old eunuch remained to atone for the crime of 30 years before.

Three days later, Guo Huai was put to death under the chopper.

Obtaining the Contract
by a Hoax

In Yidingfang outside the west gate of Kaifeng there lived two brothers named Liu. Through many years of hard work they managed to accumulate a little household property. Liu Tianxiang, the elder brother, married a woman named Yang Shi. The younger brother, Liu Tianrui, married Zhang Shi. The four of them lived together under the same roof. Liu Tianxiang had no offspring of his own, but his wife, Yang Shi, had a daughter from her first husband. A few years into his marriage, Liu Tianrui had a son and named him Liu Anzhu.

A community head called Chief Li was friendly with the Liu family. Previously, his wife and Zhang Shi were pregnant at the same time. As both families intended to strengthen their relationship, they made an agreement about the expected babies: If both turned out to be boys, they would become sworn brothers; if both turned out to be girls, they would become sworn sisters; if it turned out to be one boy and one girl, they would become husband and wife. Zhang Shi gave birth to her son, Liu Anzhu, and shortly afterward Li's wife gave birth to a daughter, named Li Dingnu. So, in accordance with the agreement, Liu Tianrui had his son formally betrothed to Chief Li's daughter. Both families were happy with the arrangement.

However, Yang Shi was a very selfish woman. She wanted her daughter to grow up and get married as soon as possible in order to get a good share of the family property. After the birth of Liu Anzhu, she began to feel

uneasy and often made caustic remarks to her sister-in-law. Fortunately, Zhang Shi had a gentle, docile temperament, and the two brothers got along quite well, so no open clash broke out in the family.

When Anzhu was three years old, a severe drought resulted in a crop failure in the area. Life became hard for the Liu family, though not to the point of starvation. Soon the imperial court issued an order. Each household must be divided in two, with half the people leaving for another place to reduce the burden in the famished area. Liu Tianxiang said to Liu Tianrui that he planned to leave home, but Tianrui disagreed. "You are older than I and not in very good health, so you should not go. Let me take my wife and son on a trip. I don't think we will have to stay away from home for too long."

Tianxiang thought for a while and nodded. "Well, one of us has to go, and the other will stay home to look after the house. Let's invite Chief Li here and make some arrangements."

When Chief Li arrived at the house, Tianxiang said to him, "I have something to tell you. This year's famine has hit very hard in this area, and the court has ordered us to reduce the number of people in each household by leaving in search of food in another place. My younger brother's family will set out in a couple of days. You are familiar with the situation in this house: We have not broken up the family and we do not want to even now. However, because of the imperial order, we have to part with each other, and it is not clear when my younger brother will return. Therefore I want to write a contract to explain the situation. My brother and I will each keep a copy of the contract. If he returns in a year or two, there will be no problem. But if something untoward should happen and make him unable to return in eight or 10 years, the contract will become a useful proof. I have asked you to come because I need you to bear witness and sign on the contract."

"Of course I will do it," consented Chief Li without difficulty.

Liu Tianxiang produced two pieces of paper and wrote the following in duplicate:

Liu Tianxiang, a resident of Yidingfang outside the west gate of Kaifeng; his younger brother, Liu Tianrui; young nephew, Liu Anzhu. Because of this year's famine, the imperial court has ordered the reduction of the number of people in each household, with some leaving the land to seek food elsewhere. My younger brother, Tianrui, volunteers to leave with his wife and son. The property of this house has never been divided. This statement is written in duplicate, with each brother keeping a copy.

This date
Drafter: Liu Tianxiang
Younger Brother: Liu Tianrui
Witness: Chief Li

The three of them signed their names, and each of the two brothers tucked away a copy of the contract.

On an auspicious date a few days later Liu Tianrui, having packed up, took leave of his elder brother and sister-in-law. The two brothers shed tears at their parting, and Chief Li came to see Tianrui off. Yang Shi, however, rejoiced inwardly as if a heavy burden had been removed from her heart.

With his wife and son, Liu Tianrui traveled along, exposed to cold and wet. One day they arrived at Xiama Village in Gaoping County, Luzhou Prefecture, Shanxi

157

Province. The area had just enjoyed a bumper harvest, and business was very brisk. Tianrui and his wife, Zhang Shi, decided to stay there, and they rented a house from a local couple, Zhang Binyi and his wife, Guo Shi. Zhang was a wealthy man with a lot of land and property in the area, but there was one thing that weighed heavily on his mind —he had no children. Zhang liked his new tenants for their diligence and cordiality and often went to talk with them. He grew to be very fond of Liu Anzhu who, at three years old, was a cute, loveable boy. When he told his wife, Guo Shi, of his intention to adopt Anzhu, she readily agreed. So they sent someone to visit Liu Tianrui and Zhang Shi with the message: "Zhang is very fond of your clever and lovely son and would like to adopt him. After that, a tie of kinship would be established between the two families. What do you think of this?"

It appeared to Liu Tianrui and Zhang Shi that such an offer from one whom they regarded as a kindhearted and wealthy man was sure to benefit their son, and they did not want to turn it down. "We would be only too glad to accept such a kind offer," they said. "Our only fear is that we will not be worthy of such a connection."

An auspicious date was chosen on which Anzhu formally became Zhang's son. His personal name was unchanged, but his family name was changed to Zhang, so from then on he was called Zhang Anzhu. Liu Tianrui's wife, Zhang Shi, acknowledged Zhang as her elder brother, and Liu Tianrui began to call him brother-in-law. Bound together by such a kinship, the two families grew to be very close. Liu Tianrui no longer needed to worry about rent or daily expenses.

About half a year passed like this. However, the happy days didn't last long. Both Liu Tianrui and his wife suddenly fell seriously ill. Zhang spared no expense in sending for doctors and buying medicines, but to no avail. A few days later, Zhang Shi died. Overwhelmed with grief, Liu Tianrui became even more ill. He called Zhang to his bed and said to him, "You are my great benefactor. I'm afraid I won't be long for this world. My wife and I have benefited a lot from your help, but we can only hope to repay your kindness in our next lives. There is something I have to tell you now."

Zhang said earnestly, "Don't speak as if we were strangers! We are like brothers to each other, so if you have anything you need done, just tell me and I will do it."

"In my hometown I have an elder brother. Before I left home, we signed a contract just in case. We made two copies, and each of us kept one. After leaving home, my wife and I came to this town and received your unbounded hospitality. Unfortunately, we are destined to die in a strange land. Anzhu is young and ignorant, but since you have adopted him, I can rest in peace. But there is something I need to ask your help about. When Anzhu grows up, please give him this copy of the contract and tell him to take the remains of my wife and me back to our hometown and bury them in our ancestral grave. This is my only wish remaining to be fulfilled. Please help me!" As he finished these words, tears rolled down his cheeks.

Zhang found it hard to speak and merely nodded repeatedly. With an effort Liu Tianrui took out the contract and handed it to Zhang, who took it without saying anything. A doctor was sent for, but Liu Tianrui was already beyond remedy. At nightfall he died.

Zhang and his wife were deeply grieved. The bodies of Liu Tianrui and his wife were placed into two coffins and buried, temporarily, in the ancestral grave of the Zhang family.

After that Zhang and his wife brought up Anzhu as

their own son. A few years later they sent him to study in the local school and paid close attention to his education. Anzhu was a clever boy gifted with a very good memory; he learned the books by reading them only once. Moreover, he was meek and modest in nature and treated his parents with great respect. Zhang and his wife loved him dearly, and the three lived together as a happy family.

Every spring and autumn Zhang and his wife would take Anzhu to the ancestral graveyard and have him kowtow to his parents' tombs without telling him why. Fifteen years later, Anzhu grew to be a lad of 18. On the Festival of Pure Brightness the couple took Anzhu to the graveyard again. Pointing to the mounds, Anzhu asked, "Father, you have me kowtow to these mounds every year, but I have never asked what relatives are buried there."

Zhang exchanged a glance with Guo Shi, and the couple fell silent. After a while Zhang sighed deeply and said, "My child, you have grown up now. We have been wanting to tell you about this, but we are afraid that you may leave us when you learn the truth."

Anzhu was confused. "What do you mean, Father?"

"Well, it's time you are told about this. We are not your natural parents. Your family name is not Zhang, nor is this place your hometown. You were named Liu, and your father was Liu Tianrui, who lived in Yidingfang outside the west gate of Kaifeng. When you were only three, your hometown was struck with famine, and the imperial court ordered the local households to reduce the number of their members. Your parents brought you here and rented a house from us. Shortly after, I adopted you as my son, and the two families became closely related as a result. Unfortunately, both your parents died of illness half a year later, and I had them buried here. That's why I bring you here every year and have you pay homage to the tombs. Herein are buried your natural parents!"

Zhang broke down in tears. Astounded, Anzhu stared at Zhang incredulously.

Zhang went on, "In your hometown you have an uncle named Liu Tianxiang. On his deathbed your father gave me a written contract concerning your family's land and property. So this is your father's last wish that he entrusted with me: When you grow up, I will inform you of your origin and tell you to return to your hometown with this contract, find your uncle and aunt, and bury the remains of your parents in their ancestral grave. My son, though we are not your natural parents, we have always treated you as our own child, the person to rely on in our last years. It is fitting and proper for you to acknowledge your natural parents, but don't forget about the past 15 years we spent together!"

As he said this, Zhang was seized with an intense sorrow. Anzhu, who had fully comprehended the import of all this, broke into tears. Falling on his knees toward his parents' tombs, he said sobbingly, "Forgive your unfilial son! He did not know his parents until today!" Overcome with distress, he swooned on the spot.

Startled, Zhang and his wife woke him up and had him carried back to the house. After a long time Anzhu's mind gradually cleared up. He said to Zhang and his wife, "Father and Mother, now that I know about this, there is no time to lose. Please give me the contract. I want to leave for Kaifeng at once with my parents' remains. As soon as I have buried them, I will return to wait on Father and Mother."

Zhang sighed. "This is what a filial son should do. You may start off tomorrow. Make the trip as short as possible to prevent us from worrying."

The following day Anzhu packed. Zhang showed him

the contract and gave it to him. The remains of Anzhu's parents were exhumed. When Anzhu was ready to leave, Zhang said to him, "My child, don't linger too long in your hometown and forget your white-haired foster parents!"

They parted in tears.

Making no delays along the way, Anzhu soon arrived in Yidingfang outside the west gate of Kaifeng. By asking around, he located the house of the Liu family and went up and knocked on the door until an old woman came out. Anzhu said, "Please, auntie, pass on a message to the head of this house. My name is Liu Anzhu, the son of Liu Tianrui. I am told this is the house of my uncle and aunt and have come here to visit them."

The old woman's face changed color when she heard this. She peered at Anzhu for a long time, and finally said, "Where are my brother and sister-in-law now? If you are Liu Anzhu, you must have a contract as proof. Otherwise how can I trust someone I have never seen before?"

"Both my parents passed away because of illness 15 years ago in Luzhou," replied Anzhu. "I was brought up by my foster parents. The contract is in my luggage."

"I am the wife of the elder Liu. Since you have brought the contract, let me look at it first."

Anzhu saluted the old woman. "I didn't know you are my aunt. Please pardon my impoliteness."

He opened his luggage, took out the contract, and handed it to the old woman. Yang Shi took it. "Wait here. I will go in and compare it with my own copy. Then I'll come back and let you in." With this she went in and closed the door behind her.

At this time, Yang Shi already had her son-in-law living in the house and wanted to leave all household property to her daughter. The last thing she wanted was the return of her brother-in-law's family. She was startled when Anzhu revealed his identity, but when she learned that both Liu Tianrui and his wife had died 15 years before, she decided not to acknowledge her nephew. Thus she went in, tucked away the contract in her pocket, and decided to ignore him. If Anzhu should come to trouble her again, she would deny having ever seen the contract.

Anzhu waited outside the door for a long time, but no one came out. It would not be proper to knock on the door again. As he was growing anxious and dejected, an old man came up to him. "Young lad, who are you? I have never seen you before. Why are you standing in front of my house?"

Anzhu looked at the old man closely before he replied, "Could you be my uncle? I am your nephew, Liu Anzhu. Fifteen years ago my parents took me to Luzhou to escape famine." He fell on his knees to salute the old man.

The old man was filled with surprise and delight. "Oh, so you are Anzhu, my child! Please get up!" Taking Anzhu by the hand, he walked into the house to the front hall. Heaving a deep sigh, he said, "My wife and I are very old, just like flickering candles. Since the three of you left, we have not heard from you for over a dozen years. It's such a joy that you can return today; you have brought new hope to the Liu family. Oh, I almost forgot. Where are your parents? Why haven't they come together with you to visit us?"

With tears in his eyes, Anzhu recounted how his parents had died of illness and how he had been brought up by his foster parents. Liu Tianxiang also became tearful on hearing the story. Wiping off his tears, he asked, "So you have brought the remains of your parents and the contract?"

"Yes. A moment ago my aunt took the contract at the door and went in to check it."

At this, Liu Tianxiang turned to call his wife. "Our nephew is here! He is waiting to meet you!"

Yang Shi came into the hall. "What nephew are you talking about?"

"Do we have another nephew? It is of course Liu Anzhu, who left with his parents in search of food 15 years ago!"

"Who is Liu Anzhu?" retorted Yang Shi. "This place is overrun with impostors who have their eyes on the little property we have. Where does this Liu Anzhu come from? Liu Anzhu's parents took a copy of the contract with them when they left. If he claims to be Anzhu, he will surely be able to show us the contract."

"Anzhu just told me he gave it to you at the door."

Yang Shi turned to Anzhu. "Really? You mean you gave it to me at the door? When was that?"

Anzhu was confounded. "Aunt, what do you mean by this? I handed the contract to you at the door just a moment ago!"

Liu Tianxiang also urged Yang Shi, "Come on, stop the joke. Take out the contract."

Yang Shi burst into rage. "Where do you want me to find the contract? I was sitting in the room all day and never took any contract from anyone at the door!"

Liu Tianxiang turned to Anzhu. "Where is the contract exactly? You must tell the truth."

Anzhu was totally confused. "How dare I lie to you, uncle? I really handed the contract to my aunt just now."

Yang Shi began to glare and curse at Anzhu. "Where do you come from, you petty beggar? Pretending to be our nephew and trying to blackmail us about the contract!"

Liu Tianxiang tried to stop her. "Don't squabble like this! If you have taken the contract, why don't you show it to me?"

Yang Shi became furious. "What a befuddled old man you are! We have been married for dozens of years, but you would rather believe this petty impostor than me! Why should I want to hide a contract of his? Do I need it to paste the window? Don't you understand? If our nephew were really here, I would be only too glad to receive him; why should I get angry over it? This petty cheat is trying to deceive us by pretending to be our nephew. He must be after our household property. Can't you see this?"

"Uncle," said Anzhu, "I am willing to renounce my share of the family property. After I have buried the remains of my parents in the family graveyard, I will return to Luzhou. I am fully capable of supporting myself in my own way."

Before Liu Tianxiang could say anything, Yang Shi shouted, "Who are you trying to deceive with such glib talk? Get out of here!" She picked up a stick and brought it down on Anzhu, causing his head to bleed. Liu Tianxiang did not move fast enough to stop her. He cried, "Don't act like this! Let's find out the truth of the matter!"

However, as he did not know his nephew by sight, and his wife adamantly denied having taken the contract, he did not know which of them to believe. So he had to let Yang Shi have her way. After beating Anzhu and driving him out of the door, Yang Shi kept on with her verbal abuses for quite a long time.

Pushed out of the house, Anzhu was so overcome with shame that he passed out. After a while he woke up. Gazing at the remains of his parents, he broke down and wept bitterly. Just then a man happened to be walking by and stopped to ask, "Young lad, what's the matter? Why are you weeping so sadly?"

"I didn't expect my uncle and aunt to be so cruel," said Anzhu. "They took the contract and refused to acknowledge me and even beat me."

The man started. "Who are you?"

"I am their nephew, Liu Anzhu. I have come from Luzhou to visit my hometown."

The man looked Anzhu up and down, then helped him to his feet. "So you are Liu Anzhu, my prospective son-in-law! I am Chief Li. Tell me the story in detail, and I will see what I can do!"

Hearing this, Anzhu saluted the old man and said in a sobbing voice, "My parents took me to Luzhou in Shanxi, where we settled down in Xiama Village in Gaoping County. We rented our house from the Zhang family. Soon afterwards, both my parents died of illness, and I was brought up by Zhang as his foster son. I was recently told of my family background, so I brought the remains of my parents here to bury them in our family's ancestral grave. However, when I visited my uncle's house today, my aunt took away the contract I had brought with me and hid it. Then she abused me, hit me with a stick, and drove me out of the house, and my head is still bleeding from the wound. How can she be so cold-blooded!"

Chief Li's face turned crimson with indignation. "You said the contract was taken away from you. But do you remember what it said?"

"Of course I do!" Anzhu then recited the contents of the contract without missing a word. Chief Li was convinced. "You are doubtlessly my future son-in-law. That wicked woman was so unreasonable! I will knock on their door and go in to reason with them. If she changes her mind, everything will be all right. If not, we can lodge a case against her at the yamen in Kaifeng. I don't think she will succeed in denying your share of the family property in this way!"

Chief Li went up and knocked on the door. As soon

as he saw the couple, he blurted out, "My in-laws, why did you refuse to acknowledge your nephew and hit him on the head?"

Yang Shi said, "You are misinformed about this, Chief. That ruffian was an impostor trying to rob us of our money. If he were our nephew, he would have the contract which bears your signature. But he has absolutely nothing to prove his identity. How can we believe him?"

"He said you took the contract from him and hid it away. Why do you deny this?"

"This is ridiculous, Chief! Where did I see him before? How could I take the contract from him? This is just a story he made up. You'd better not meddle in this, Chief!" She picked up the stick to strike at Anzhu again, but Chief Li shielded Anzhu and pulled him out of the house. "What a wicked old woman!" he said. "Does she really think she can get away with all this? Don't worry, my child. Tomorrow we will hand in a complaint to the *yamen* in Kaifeng. Lord Bao will certainly give a just verdict!"

Early the next morning, Chief Li wrote a complaint and went with Anzhu to the *yamen* in Kaifeng. When Lord Bao took his seat in the principal hall, the two of them began crying "injustice!" outside. Lord Bao took the written complaint, read it over, and ordered Chief Li to come up and tell the story. After hearing him out, Lord Bao said, "I think you are instigating the boy to bring up a false charge!"

"Your Excellency, please listen to me! He is indeed my betrothed son-in-law. I have come here to complain on his behalf because I will be his father-in-law, and also because I signed my name to the contract as a witness. I have never brought up a false charge against anyone. How dare I deceive Your Excellency in such a grave matter!"

"Did you recognize your future son-in-law then?"

"He left home at three years of age and returned only yesterday. I could not recognize him."

"If you could not recognize him, and he had no contract to prove his identity, why do you believe his words?"

"The contract is known only to the Liu brothers and myself. This boy knew the contents of the contract by heart without missing a word. I could not but believe him!"

Lord Bao thought for a while, then ordered Chief Li to be taken away and Liu Anzhu brought up. When questioned, Anzhu recounted what had happened to him. The wound on his head was examined. Lord Bao asked, "You must tell me the truth. Are you pretending to be from the Liu family in order to get some of the family property?"

"Your Excellency," Anzhu replied, "I beg you to listen to me! What is false can never pass for true. How could I bring myself to fabricate a story about my own origin? What's more, Zhang, my foster father, has enough land and property to last me an entire lifetime; there is really no need for me to seek after ill-gotten gains. I already said that I would renounce my share of the family property. I only want my uncle and aunt to acknowledge me as their nephew and allow me to bury the remains of my parents in our ancestral grave. After that, I will return to live with my foster father in Luzhou. Your Excellency, please find out the truth!"

Lord Bao found the words of Chief Li and Anzhu reasonable, so he accepted their complaint and sent runners to summon Liu Tianxiang and his wife.

The couple arrived at the *yamen*. After the runners announced the opening of the court with a loud shout, Liu Tianxiang was brought into the main hall. Lord Bao asked, "Liu Tianxiang, let me ask you a question. Do you have a nephew?"

"Yes, Your Excellency, I have a nephew named Liu Anzhu. Fifteen years ago his parents left with him for another place in search of food."

"Take a good look now. Is the young man over there you nephew?"

Liu Tianxiang looked up and saw the young man who had been beaten by his wife the day before. He hastily replied, "Your Excellency, this young lad came to my house yesterday and claimed to be my nephew. I was only too glad to have my nephew back, but as I had not seen him for 15 years, I could not be sure if this was really him. And this lad didn't have the contract with him. So I could not make up my mind."

"He said he has given the contract to your wife."

"Your Excellency, this is exactly what I am puzzling over. He says with absolute certainty that he has brought the contract and has given it to my wife, but my wife says with absolute certainty that she has never seen him before. I don't know what to think, so please, Your Excellency, find out the truth about this!"

Lord Bao found Liu Tianxiang's words confused but earnest, so he nodded his head and bade him be taken aside. Yang Shi was brought forth.

Yang Shi began to bawl tearfully how she was wronged. She berated Anzhu, saying he was an imposter who had falsely accused her after failing to deceive her. She lamented that an old woman like her should suffer such public humiliation because of recriminations from a little ruffian, and pleaded with Lord Bao to help her.

Lord Bao considered for a moment, then suddenly banged his wooden block on the table. "Well, what a deceitful couple!"

Turning to Anzhu, he said, "Since your uncle and aunt

have behaved in such a heartless manner toward you, there is nothing more to say. Now I will allow you to give each of them 10 strokes of the birch, on the spot, in order to revenge the beating you suffered and to warn others against following their example."

Flabbergasted, Anzhu fell to his knees and pleaded, "Your Excellency, I dare not do that! They are after all my uncle and aunt. I have handed in my complaint not to take revenge or to fight for the family property. All I want is a clear judgement so that I can acknowledge my ancestors and bury my parents' remains in our ancestral grave. I dare not act against the elders of my family!"

Hearing this, Lord Bao became clear about the case. He pulled a long face and smiled coldly. "Do you think I can be deceived by a young lad like you? Do you think I will believe you to be the nephew of the Liu family just because you pretend to be respectful to your superiors? Do you think you can achieve your aim fortuitously just by claiming you don't want a share of the family property but just want to acknowledge your ancestors? Runners, take this impostor and throw him into prison! I will interrogate him on another day, and mete out due punishment to be a warning to the likes of him!"

Anzhu and Chief Li were taken completely by surprise. Anzhu reacted more quickly and began shouting "injustice!" But the runners came up and dragged him away.

Lord Bao said to the Liu couple and Chief Li, "The case is clear. The young man is a very wily impostor. The moral degeneration of the world is getting worse every day; I will punish him severely to warn others against following his example. You may leave now and wait for my summons."

Yang Shi felt relieved and delighted. "Little ruffian, don't blame me for this!" she thought to herself. "You asked for it. Trying to sue me! Well, you end up in prison yourself. It's fine for me. I no longer have to worry about you."

After retreating from the hall, Lord Bao sent for a prison guard and gave him a few words of instruction. He then sent runners to Luzhou to summon Zhang Bingyi.

It was in a state of perplexity that Chief Li left the *yamen* for home that day. He no longer knew for sure if the young lad was really his prospective son-in-law. Despite that, he often went to the *yamen* to make inquiries. One day the prison guard said to him impatiently, "He is dying! What's the use of your asking? His Excellency no longer needs to try him. His wound has become infected. He won't last for more than a few days!"

Chief Li felt dazed at this news. He then went back and told the Liu couple about it. Liu Tianxiang made no comment, but Yang Shi remarked, "He asked for it. He has no one else to blame!"

A few days later, both the Liu couple and Chief Li were summoned by the *yamen*.

Ushered into the hall, they kowtowed in salute to Lord Bao, who bade them stand aside. Pointing to a white-haired old man, Lord Bao said, "There is indeed a Zhang Bingyi in Luzhou, and he is here. He has testified that his foster son is the natural son of Liu Tianrui and nephew of Liu Tianxiang, and that he has seen the contract himself. He also confirmed that Liu Anzhu has returned to his hometown to pay homage to his ancestors."

Yang Shi said, "But we have not seen our nephew for many years, so the only reliable proof is the contract. Without the contract, we cannot believe any of this."

"Your words are quite reasonable," said Lord Bao. "Zhang Bingyi's attestment is far from convincing."

Turning to the runners, he ordered, "Bring that young lad here!"

The runner went out and returned quickly. "Your Excellency," he said, "he is dying of a severe illness and can hardly move."

"What?" Lord Bao glared at him. "He can hardly move? Do you want me to go and see him? Bring him here!"

The runner kept on repeating "yes" and hurried away. Shortly afterward, he returned with the prison guard, who reported to Lord Bao, "Your Excellency, the prisoner has just died of illness!"

Surprised, Lord Bao asked, "He's dead? How did he die? Let the postmortem examiner investigate and report to me at once."

At the news brought by the prison guard, Zhang Bingyi passed out on the spot. Liu Tianxiang and Chief Li stared at each other in bewilderment. Yang Shi put her hand on her forehead and heaved a sigh, not saying a word.

It was very quiet in the hall. A short while later, the examiner came. "Your Excellency, I have checked the body. It is a boy about 18 years old; his head was injured by something hard, and an infection resulted and caused his death. The area around the dead man's temples are bruised from the wound."

Lord Bao fell silent for a moment. Then he said, "Well, look at what we have here. The man's dead. This case is now more serious." He looked down at Yang Shi. "Didn't you beat him?"

"Your Excellency," Yang Shi said anxiously, "I did beat him. Well, it was purely an accident that I—"

"You don't need to find excuses for yourself!" Lord Bao interrupted her impatiently. "You beat him, and he is now dead, so I must hold you responsible for it. Let me ask again: That lad, who is now dead, is he really not your nephew?"

"Your Excellency, he is really not my nephew!"

"Well," Lord Bao seemed to be considering. "In that case you are in big trouble. If the lad and you belonged to the same family, you would be guilty of killing a junior family member by mistake, and the penalty would be no more than a fine. Since you are not related, the case is a serious one. You must have heard the saying, 'One who borrows must pay the forfeit with his money, but one who murders must pay the forfeit with his life!' If he was a mere stranger, why didn't you just drive him away? Why did you hit him on the head? Well, he died of an infection from the injury you gave him. The law is absolutely clear about this: Whoever has committed battery resulting in death must pay with his life!"

Having said this, Lord Bao roared an order to the runners, "Seize the old woman, lock her up in chains and throw her into prison to await execution in autumn!"

The runners uttered a loud cry and carried over a heavy iron chain. Shuddering in horror, her face turning livid, Yang Shi began wailing loudly, "I am wronged! I am wronged!"

"How could you be wronged?" demanded Lord Bao harshly.

Yang Shi went up and kneeled. "Your Excellency, he is my nephew ... my nephew of lineal descent."

Lord Bao smiled coldly. "Are you out of your mind? You beat him to death because he pretended to be your nephew. Why do you say he is your nephew?"

"Your Excellency, he is really my nephew!"

"I didn't believe his wily words, so how can I believe yours? What proof do you have?"

"Your Excellency, the contract ... I did take the contract from him. I have it here."

She fumbled inside her clothes and brought out the contract, which she handed up to Lord Bao.

Lord Bao read the contract, put it down, and said to Yang Shi, "If you had known this day must come, you would have repented of your mistake long since! You have nearly ruined your family by your selfishness and greed. Being too smart is no good for you. Now that you acknowledge him to be your nephew, you must take back his body and make no more trouble!"

Yang Shi could only say "yes" repeatedly. Lord Bao ordered the prison guard, "Bring Liu Anzhu here!"

The guard went away and returned with Liu Anzhu walking behind him. People in the hall were astounded and more than ever confused. Liu Anzhu was dressed in fine clothes and had a ruddy complexion; the wound on his forehead had already healed. He walked up to Lord Bao and kowtowed. "Your Excellency, thank you so much for telling right from wrong and restoring my family name!"

Lord Bao handed him the contract, a smile flickering on his lips. "I appreciate your filial piety and adherence to the principles of righteousness, so I set up this trap to get back the contract for you. Take this and keep it in a safe place. And keep your forehead from the stick!"

Anzhu thanked Lord Bao again and took the contract.

Yang Shi realized what had happened. Kneeling with her head down, she was overwhelmed with shame.

Lord Bao took up the brush and wrote the verdict: "An honor will be conferred on the family of Liu Anzhu, who deserves recommendation for his filial devotion. The remains of Liu Tianrui and his wife are allowed to be buried in their ancestral grave. Chief Li must select a proper date to marry his daughter to Liu Anzhu. Liu Tianxiang, though muddle-headed, is spared on account of his old age. Yang Shi deserves a severe punishment; however, because her victim, Liu Anzhu, has pleaded on her behalf, she will be freed after paying a fine. The property of the Liu family will be inherited by Liu Anzhu."

Thus Yang Shi, for all her calculation and scheming, ended up ruining the future of her own daughter. After the trial everyone returned home. Zhang Bingyi, after paying a visit to Liu Tianxiang, returned to Luzhou. After Liu Anzhu had his parents' remains buried in the ancestral grave, a wedding was held for him and Chief Li's daughter. A month later, the young couple returned to Luzhou to take care of Anzhu's foster parents.

As for the contract, Liu Anzhu burned it before the tombs of his parents.

图书在版编目(CIP)数据

狸猫换太子:包公断案故事:英文/胡本编.—北京:外文出版社,1997

ISBN 7-119-01896-5

Ⅰ.狸… Ⅱ.胡… Ⅲ.民间故事-作品集-中国-英文 Ⅳ.I277.3

中国版本图书馆 CIP 数据核字 (97) 第 07885 号

狸猫换太子

——包公断案故事

胡 本 编

责任编辑 贾先锋

装帧设计 朱振安

插图绘制 李士仮

*

©外文出版社

外文出版社出版

(中国北京百万庄大街 24 号)

邮政编码 100037

北京外文印刷厂印刷

中国国际图书贸易总公司发行

(中国北京车公庄西路 35 号)

北京邮政信箱第 399 号 邮政编码 100044

1997 年(36 开)第 1 版

1997 年第 1 版第 1 次印刷

(英)

ISBN 7-119-01896-5 /I·434(外)

01650

10-E-3116P